Christmas
at
Sugarplum
Falls

Christmas at Sugarplum Falls

SUGARPLUM FALLS BOOK ONE

JENNIFER GRIFFITH

Christmas at Sugarplum Falls

ISBN: 9798491985197

This is a work of fiction. Names, characters, places, and events are creations of the author's imagination or are used fictitiously. Any resemblance to actual persons, living or dead, events, or locations, is purely coincidental.

Cover art credit: Blue Water Books, 2021

For Penny

"Friendship is a sheltering tree." –Samuel Taylor Coleridge

Chapter 1

Claire

"Remind me why you're doing this again?" Portia sat on Claire Downing's kitchen counter swinging her legs and chomping on a stray piece of celery that didn't make it into the stuffing. "Thanksgiving was just a few days ago. Slaving all day to make a holiday meal—not on an official holiday, mind you—for people Mayor Lang told you to invite over? People we don't even know?"

Heavenly holiday scents of sage, thyme, and rosemary, along with roasting turkey, wafted through Claire's kitchen in her red-brick house on Apricot Avenue. It hadn't smelled this good in here since Mom and the girls moved out three years ago.

"We probably know some of them. I know you. You're bringing Owen. It won't exactly be a roomful of strangers." Other than her longtime best friends and Claire, it might not be a roomful of anyone. Despite good recommendations from Mayor Lang, most of Claire's invitations had gone unanswered. Seriously, who turned down turkey dinner?

All I need to do is meet a few new people.

"But remind me of the *why* again." Portia jumped off the counter and

1

started scrubbing a few dishes in the sink. "It's a ton of work and expense, if you ask me."

Claire cracked the oven door and reached in with a turkey baster to help the bird stay moist and scrumptious for when her guests came. "The why is that my mother issued me a challenge"—after hearing Claire pine for family visits over the phone one time too many. "She insists I try something new."

"Then watch a horror movie or test out a new restaurant. Finally show the world your clothing designs, for heaven's sake."

Claire cringed. *Try something new* was Mom's code for *quit hiding your designs. Be brave.* "Not yet."

"Fine, but why the slaving all day in a kitchen to feed strangers—who may or may not even like watching your Christmas movies or putting on your Christmas-themed skits after the pumpkin pie is served?"

Pie! "Thanks for reminding me." Claire tugged two cartons of heavy whipping cream from the refrigerator. "Do you know how to whip cream?"

"Me?" Portia chortled. "I don't think you want to risk your cream investment on me."

Maybe not. Portia was more decorative than useful when it came to the kitchen, but she was fun. And Claire did enjoy decoration in life. It was nice, at least, to have someone around for when fun things went on.

Since her family had moved away and left Claire in Sugarplum Falls.

And sure, it was cool that Portia and Owen had gotten together. Great, even. To suddenly have her two best friends dating at least lessened the "third wheel" feeling Claire always seemed to suffer from. They'd invited her on picnics in the spring, to the fireworks in the summer, and spent most weekends hanging out at her house or near the falls or doing stuff together.

Claire whipped the cream. She also went over the skit ideas in her mind again. Would guests refuse to play along? Oh, maybe this whole thing was a terrible idea.

"Ding-dong." Owen banged through the back door. In one arm he held a large box labeled Kingston Orchards. In the other, he toted a sack from the grocery store, setting them both on Claire's countertop with his huge smile. "I come bearing apples. I hope you like Granny Smith. They're best for pie. And

2

as requested, I brought ice. Is twenty pounds enough?"

Portia dove for him, affecting a swoon. "Owen Kingston, look at you carrying all those heavy things." She patted his biceps. "Take off that coat and show us those guns." She peeled away his leather jacket and more or less forced him to flex his muscles.

Yeah, they did strain nicely against the hems of his t-shirt's sleeves. "Impressive," Claire said. "You must work out."

"I work out. Meaning I work *outside*." Owen put his coat on the same hook he'd used for almost twenty years. "What can I do to help?"

"You can use those *guns* of yours to pull the turkey out of the oven for me. I think we have about two minutes left until perfection." Claire handed Portia a water pitcher to add some of Owen's ice offering to. "And then carve?"

"Carving meat. Manly job." Owen chose a knife from the block. "Who else is coming over?"

Smirking, Portia shook ice into one of the goblets. "It's a holiday surprise."

With a tilt of his head, Owen asked, "Really, Claire? I thought—"

"I invited twenty, and I cooked for thirty." Just to be safe. Mayor Lang's list of people in Sugarplum Falls who might not have anyone to spend Christmas with wasn't very long, so Claire had just extended her invitation to everyone on it. "I probably should have asked for RSVPs or something."

"Ya think?" Portia snorted.

The oven timer rang. "When food is involved, yeah." Owen located oven mitts and pulled the turkey out. His muscles did flex nicely.

Better, Owen really was a great guy. In fact, he never even showed annoyance while he dated Portia Sutherland to have her less-sparkling sidekick in tow all the time. How could he ever advance the relationship with Claire always in the room?

Weirdly, Portia didn't seem to mind, either. Claire was the only one hating that she was preventing something good from becoming more serious.

This is why I need to find another batch of friends. Please, someone, show up for dinner.

"Seems like too much food, even for a Kingston family get-together."

"It's because Claire is *trying something new.*" Portia handed Owen the platter for the carved meat. "Her mom *challenged* her. That's why we're stuck doing this."

"You're calling eating a gourmet turkey dinner *stuck* doing something?" Owen expertly placed the drumstick whole on the platter. Everyone loved seeing the drumstick kept intact. "I call it fantastic."

"You just like food."

"I'm a guy."

Still, *thanks, Owen, for the backup.* "Look, I'm appeasing my mom. It was her suggestion—a supper club. I'm kicking it off with a big meal, just to draw people in. Then, when people feel comfortable and get to know each other, we can all take turns hosting. I'm aiming for about a dozen people in all."

Imagine *twelve* friends emerging from the Sugarplum Falls woodwork. People who weren't already caught in their own families' obligations like everyone Claire already knew. How would that be? Imagine having people to actually go with to all of the amazing Christmas events planned in Sugarplum Falls. But every year it was the same at the holidays, with Portia spending every night at practice for the town Christmas play, and Claire stuck choosing to go alone or not at all to the Hot Cocoa Festival or the Waterfall Lights, or any of the other festivities.

That's why this supper club thing had to work—and why she'd finally caved to Mom's urging.

Owen expelled a sigh. "Man, I don't even get how people have time for friends. Other than you two, of course."

"Right?" Portia snitched a piece of the white meat. "Family obligations every single weekend."

"Look who's proving my mother's point." Ugh.

"Hey, remember that Sutherland status isn't all parties and laughter." Portia waved a *pshaw* hand. "Make Sugarplum Falls the *best.* Serve, serve, serve. It's exhausting. Do you know how much I just want to be like my uncle Zeke and be the black sheep of the family? I should go off to New York City

4

and star in a musical. Or Los Angeles. Or anywhere."

Here came the old threat. Someday she might make good on it. Claire shuddered.

"For now, you get to star in the town Christmas play." Owen pressed a consoling kiss to her temple. It was still a little weird sometimes to see. "And you'll dazzle."

"Dazzle. In the town Christmas play." Portia guffawed. "Should I be the one to point out the elephant in the room, or does someone else want to? That play is smellier than bleu cheese."

"Yes, but it's the only play we have for now. Besides"—Owen placed an arm over her shoulder—"your acting elevates it."

Owen was so perfect for Portia. He could bring her down to earth when no one else could. Such a great guy. Not half bad as a friend, either, if not a boyfriend. Which, he'd never be for Claire. They'd friend-zoned each other for far too long.

"Elevate it. Ha! From negative level a thousand to negative nine hundred ninety-nine." Portia squirmed. "I really should have gotten brave and tried L.A.'s acting scene."

Owen enfolded her in his arms, guns a-blazin'. "I, for one, am glad you stayed." He pulled her head against his broad chest.

The public display of affection continued, and Claire looked away, but she was glad Portia had stayed, too. *Everyone I'm close to leaves.*

"Tell you what, Portia." Owen leaned back and forth with Portia in his arms. "I'll do whatever I can to help you be glad you stayed in Sugarplum Falls."

"You really mean that?" Portia looked up at him, her eyes shining. She really did have acting chops—probably because she felt every single emotion acutely. "I'm holding you to it." She grinned fiercely and gave a maniacal laugh.

Yikes. She'd better not be planning something terrible. Portia had planned a few terrible things in the past. It was how Claire had ended up eating a bug once. Luckily, she'd learned her lesson early—unlike Owen, apparently.

"Knock-knock!" A man's voice came from the front room, and the front

5

door clicked shut. "Does this house that smells like Thanksgiving and Christmas dinners collided belong to Claire Downing, my high school friend?"

The stentorian bass voice was unmistakable.

"Archie?" Portia mouthed. "You invited Archie Holdaway?" Portia shot Claire one of those *nooooo!* looks she was famous for.

"Um … ?" Claire had just copied and pasted Mayor Lang's list and printed labels, barely looking at them at all. She should have seen Archie's name and deleted it. Fast. "Hey," she said, hustling into her front room, where the Christmas tree blinked and a few candles burned. "It's so good to see you." She shook his hand heartily. "It's been a long time."

"I've been so buried in the high school teaching job I haven't poked my head out to see anyone since I got back to town in late summer." His voice lingered on the *anyone,* and his eyes lingered on Portia. "But I should have. Good to see you guys." He only looked at Portia.

Claire's mistake was a humongous oversight. This could go very badly. Unless—"Archie, you remember Owen Kingston?"

"Sure." Archie still gawped at Portia.

"He's Portia's boyfriend"—Claire emphasized *boyfriend*—"of about a year." Not quite, but since about the time Owen's Granddad died—and … the accident.

Archie tore his eyes off Portia and aimed the gaze at Owen. His face went from simpering to scowling. If ever she was short on funds, Claire should offer to have him over for poker night, just so she could clean him out.

"Kingston Orchards. Right."

The air thickened—unlike Claire's turkey gravy. This was so bad. Owen shot Claire a look that said *what do we do?*

She shrugged. *Help me?* she mouthed.

Owen nodded and threw his hands together. "It's a quarter after." A loud clap snapped everyone back to attention. "The turkey is carved, shall we sit down to eat?" He moved to the table and held out a chair. "Claire, do you have seating assignments in mind?"

"Anywhere you like." With twenty places set but only four guests, this wasn't turning out to be much of a club. Unless she called it The Awkward

Dinner Reunion Club.

Portia sat down first, at the wall-end, as if to scoot as far from Archie as possible. Alas, Archie jumped and chose the chair closest to her—then slid it even closer. Now there was no way for Owen to seat himself beside Portia, and her annoyance showed. Archie slid even nearer.

Owen cleared his throat and shot Claire a droll look. Ugh. If only turkey drippings in the oven would set off the fire alarm and put them all out of their misery.

They found seats across from the others, Owen beside Claire. As he lowered into his chair, his shoulder brushed against hers, and she glanced down at it. The triceps were on full display. Working outside all summer in the orchards really did turn his upper arms into guns. The kind from action movies.

Not that Claire was scoping him out. Sheesh, he was dating her best friend. However, she could appreciate good form. Claire was a patron of the arts, including sculpture. Like Owen's musculature. *And let's not leave out his jaw line.*

"You're teaching at the high school?" Claire asked after they'd said grace. "What subjects?"

Archie had left Sugarplum Falls for the teaching college at the same time Claire and Portia had left for college. Now, running her shop, she didn't see many men. Men did not hang out at Apple Blossom Boutique. Well, other than Owen, who showed up now and then with Portia or to bring Claire a drink from The Cider Press if he was downtown.

"English, but they are trying to get me to start a drama department. I told them I had my hands full with the town Christmas play."

Portia's head snapped upward from staring down at her green bean casserole. "You're in the play? Auditions haven't happened yet. How—?"

"I'm not in it. I'm directing it. At Mayor Lang's insistence."

Owen chortled. "Yeah, the mayor of Sugarplum Falls can be insistent."

"Highly," Claire said. Mayor Lisa Lang kept hounding Claire about participating in her dating match-up activity at the upcoming Hot Cocoa Festival. Claire was ignoring her calls. "That's great, Archie. Maybe you can help it move along at a little faster clip this year."

7

Owen muttered something beside Claire that sounded like *Two hours of torture is what they should officially title it.* "Good for you, helping out the town," he said more audibly. "Anything I can do to help, let me know."

"Yes. Owen is great at everything. He used to own a construction company before he inherited Kingston Orchard last year," Portia said.

"I haven't inherited it."

Claire cringed for him. He hadn't inherited it yet. Owen's dad was still alive. Technically.

"I'm managing." To say more would be a buzzkill.

Not that there was much buzz to kill. This supper club was the most DOA thing in this house since Owen pulled Claire's turkey out of the oven.

"Try out for the play, Portia." Archie pointed his turkey-lanced fork at her.

"I don't know, Archie." Why was she playing coy? It wasn't like Portia Sutherland *wouldn't* audition for the only dramatic performance in Sugarplum Falls. "I've done it the last three years. I've starred, you know."

"I know!" Archie's turkey flipped from his fork under the force of his enthusiastic reply. It landed atop the cranberry jelly, which was still shaped like the can. "I need someone experienced!"

"There you go, Portia. Now you've got it—a reason to be glad you stuck around for the season instead of heading off to New York or L.A. or wherever." Owen took a forkful of stuffing and crunched the celery in it. "This is really good, Claire." He took another bite before finishing the first, a visible compliment.

"You were planning on leaving?" Archie looked stricken. "Are you serious?"

It was amazing how Portia, with nothing more than the bat of an eye or the lifting of a brow could convey almost any emotion. This time it was disinterest. "Like Owen said, I needed a reason to stay." She gave Owen one of those luscious smiles that no man could ever resist, at least not for as long as Claire had known Portia, which was most of her life. "As if Owen wasn't enough of a reason. You're too good to me, Owen."

Cue the red, wrinkling forehead on Archie. Geez, what was his problem?

He was the one who'd dropped Portia back in the day. Regretting his decision?

"Owen," Archie muttered. "Owen Kingston. Geez."

Portia slammed her fork onto the side of her china dish—the good kind for special occasions from the upstairs cupboard. "Are you going to stop that forehead wrinkling or what, Archie?" The spoon clattered like an exclamation point.

"Stop what?"

"Stop being like that!" Portia got up and shoved her cloth napkin onto her plate. "If you're going to simper and be a beast, you can just forget about me trying out for the Christmas play." She stormed out of the room.

Archie chased after her. "Portia! Wait!"

So much for a friendly dinner.

Chapter 2

Owen

So much for a friendly dinner. Owen slid a sideways glance at Claire, who was frowning at her pool of gravy atop the untouched potatoes.

"I'm sorry about Portia." He stabbed at his own gravy, and a little rivulet spilled over the potato causeway.

"You don't have to apologize for her to me. She's my best friend." Claire got up and began clearing the dishes. "And I'm the one who accidentally invited someone who'd get under her skin."

Yeah, but that was a case of way more than getting under Portia's skin. She was downright pulling histrionics. Sure, the woman was a drama addict, but—"Usually she keeps the drama on the stage." Owen got up to help. "Dinner was good. You're a good cook."

"The food was good, even if dinner wasn't." Claire's voice was flat. "It's strange how the food tastes different based on ambience, don't you think?"

"And by ambience, you mean the company." Dinner would have tasted a lot better tonight if that Archie dude hadn't showed up and turned everything sour. What was his problem? Owen didn't remember the guy, probably since he'd been a year older in school than Portia and Claire—and whoever that girlfriend-disturbing teacher was. "I guess we'll eat pie another time."

More's the pity. Pie was the best part. He rinsed a plate.

10

"Speak for yourself. I'm having pie now, with or without anyone else." Claire pulled two kinds of pie from the refrigerator, cut a slice of each, and doused them with whipped cream dollops. "The whipped cream to pie ratio should be about three to one."

She offered both to Owen, and he accepted the berry crumble.

"I couldn't agree more." The pie was even better than the turkey and gravy, but that might be due to Claire's theory about ambience. Lack of Archie Holdaway brought out the tart sweetness. "Blackberries?"

"And raspberries." She took a bite of pumpkin pie. "Mmm. I'm actually glad twenty people didn't show up. Now I have breakfast for a week. Pumpkin—is it a fruit or a vegetable?"

"Both." Owen reached his fork over to her plate. "May I?" She allowed it, and he took a bite. "Mmm. Just the right amount of cloves. Well played."

"I do like to dial up the spice." Claire suddenly blushed. "No double-entendre intended."

"No double-entendre taken." But that was cute. Claire was always cute. And comfortable. She was the sorbet between courses of jalapeño poppers and spicy jerk chicken. "What do you know about that Archie person in there?" He aimed a thumb over his shoulder toward the living room where Portia had gone. "I'm sensing a history."

"Oh, there's a history." Claire waved a forkful of whipped cream. "A messy one. They dated, but it ended a long time ago. They were in drama classes together."

Drama guy. No wonder Owen hadn't known him in school. Sports had fully occupied the hours that the family business or academics hadn't sucked up. The only reason he knew Claire back then was they ended up sitting together in a few classes. Claire had been understated as always, and a stealth-genius at world geography which Owen had been retaking after failing his freshman year, so he'd asked to study with her. A friendship had grown slowly. Organically.

Even better, Claire was never throwing herself at Owen, then or now. Being not just a school-renowned athlete but also the heir-apparent of the Kingston Orchard had its downsides. Claire had been easy to trust. Still was.

11

"Ah, Portia's dramatic past," he said. Now there appeared to be Portia's dramatic present, too. However, with any luck the girl had a less dramatic future. "If there are details I need to know, you'll tell me, right?"

"You can count on me, captain." Claire saluted with her fork, transferring a little blop of white onto a spot of fair skin just above her eyebrow.

Owen couldn't leave it there. He stepped forward and, with the side of his thumb, gently removed it. "I know I can."

Claire froze, and her gaze tilted up toward his fingers, which were still perched in the air near her forehead.

He dropped his hand to his side. "Sorry. There was some whipped cream." Why was his mouth suddenly dry? He turned away and wiped the cream on his thigh.

Geez. What was he doing touching Claire's face?

Well, it was Claire, his longtime friend, recent best friend. Besides, who could look anywhere else when Portia was on the scene? She upstaged entire populations of humanity. Meeting her through Claire when he came back to Sugarplum Falls to manage the orchard had been the pleasantest of several whirlwinds at a time when his life was being whirled beyond recognition.

"So, Claire." He grabbed a water glass to get a drink to cool his face. "What are you doing for Christmas?" Better to re-inject some normalcy in the air. "Got any plans?"

She thawed from her frozen state. "This was it."

"What was?"

"This supper club. I was going to cultivate a social group so that I'd have people to spend the holidays with." She placed uneaten dinner rolls in a plastic bag. "Like I said, everyone else in town has family. Mine moved away."

"But Portia and I hang out with you, right?"

"You're dating. Each other. I'm ..."

Oh. Right. It might be weird to be Claire in this situation. "I mean, just because tonight didn't work out, doesn't mean it never will. Why not try again?"

Claire took her last bite of pie. "What are your plans?" She sidestepped the supper club topic and obviously closed it.

12

"The usual Kingston family mayhem, but I was also serious about doing whatever I can to help Portia want to stick around." If Portia had a huge success, then she might be willing to exit stage left on a high note and start a new phase of life. With him. Or else at least they could finally make time to date seriously enough to decide whether they worked.

"You mean help with the play? You've *seen* the play, right?" Claire dropped her chin and stared up at him, looking like she might gag. "The best thing you could do for that play is to burn down the Kingston Theater."

"Everyone knows it's bad. But it's tradition. Christmas means tradition." Not that he wanted to watch the play, even with Portia as the star, but it mattered to his girlfriend, so it should matter to Owen. "Even if it's corny, it's togetherness."

Claire ran hot water in the sink and added dish soap. "What's the Kingston mayhem you mentioned? The usual? Family games and gift exchanges and eating too much?"

"Yeah, well, this year has been anything but usual." Owen picked up a dish rag, and they fell into an easy routine of wash, dry, put away. The Downing house kitchen was so orderly, everything went somewhere obvious. It was his second-favorite kitchen in the world.

"First Christmas without Granddad Kingston."

"It'll be a year next month." Nobody was handling it very well. Especially not Owen, who'd caused the worst-case-scenario for the Kingston family. Stupid carelessness. Worse than worst, it'd happened right in the orchard soon after Granddad's funeral.

And then the in-fighting had begun, and it hadn't ended. Disputes about the orchard, how to best run it, mostly, but lots of other squabbles.

The Kingstons were more or less at war.

And every bitter word could be traced back to Owen's momentary carelessness. The accident. Rumblings of disunity were rocking the extended family's foundations.

Oh, Dad. *If Heaven will let you wake up from that coma, I swear, the first thing I'll do is apologize.*

Worse, without Dad, the Kingstons were stuck with Owen as their stand-

13

in patriarch of the orchards, when they all silently blamed him. The whole thing was sickening.

Nothing he did to try to make up for it could ever be enough. No, the Kingston family holidays were bound to be anything but festive. More like tense and fraught with suspicion.

"Holidays can really be the worst," Claire said.

"Kingstons always muddle through." Until the unprecedented now.

I need to be the one to pull us together, but since I'm the one who broke us apart, who's going to follow my lead?

Claire stopped washing. The hot water still poured, but she held still. Finally, she looked up at Owen. "What if ..."

Owen set the plate he'd dried on its shelf. "What if what?"

"Never mind. I'd be interfering. Forget it."

"Just say it. We're friends, so it's not interfering." Claire had never pressured him—or probably anyone else. Of course, Owen wasn't exactly the type to allow himself to be pressured into doing something he didn't want to do—unless he was duty-bound. As in the case of accepting the leadership reins of Kingston Orchard. "Shoot."

Claire shut off the water and turned to lean her back against the sink. "What if you were to do something new?"

"Uh, that's your mom's challenge for you. Are you trying to play tag-you're-it, handing it off to me, like cooties?"

A smile showed all her white teeth against her peach-pink lipstick. "Very funny." She ran her hands through her long strawberry blonde hair and tousled it, making it fall in loose waves at her shoulders. She couldn't be more strikingly different from Portia, whose raven hair was cut into a sharp, short bob at chin-length, and whose eyes were dark and piercing, in contrast to her olive skin. Everything about Claire gave off a pinkish hue, like a sunset's glow.

Why am I analyzing this? Because he analyzed things. That was why. Nothing wrong with making assessments about his good friend's appearance. Honestly, his *best* friend these days, since all his non-relatives had either married or moved off to Caldwell City.

"What's your idea for something new? Hit me with it."

14

Claire opened her mouth, but a scraping of wood-against-wood snapped him to wakefulness, as Portia pushed her way past the dining room into the kitchen.

"Tell him I'm not doing the play, Owen." She was followed by Archie, who looked as if someone had just replaced his Christmas stocking with a dirty gym sock. "Tell him since the Kingston Theater had a flood, and all the sets and costumes are ruined, that I'm not getting up on that stage and humiliating myself with warped scenery and mildewed dresses."

"There was a flood?" In his family's namesake theater? "When?"

But neither of the drama people answered.

"But, Portia!" Archie was practically on his knees. Portia could do that to men, for sure. "I'm telling you, I'm going to make the play better. I swear it. I even got Mayor Lang's approval to change some things."

"The play's smelly essence is the same, Archie. You said so yourself. The same stinky storyline, and add to that stinky flood-damage, stinky costumes, stinky sets? There's really no choice but to cancel. Let a dead tradition be buried. Rest in peace, town Christmas play." She brushed her hands against her thighs, as if dusting off the ashes of the play's cremated corpse. "Mayor Lang will understand."

"Pah!" An explosion came from Claire, who was washing dishes again. "Mayor Lang? Understand logic—when town tradition is on the line? We all know that's the most ludicrous statement of the day."

"See, Portia?" Archie clung to Portia's arm. "It's happening with or without you. I need it to happen with you. Please?"

The skin on the back of Owen's neck bunched up in a *hands off my woman* reaction—though he should be used to it by now. When a guy's girlfriend starred in plays, he had to be patient, because she often had to feign affection for—and be pawed by—other men.

Owen hadn't gotten used to it. Hopefully it would end soon.

"Forget it. It's like I told Owen and Claire earlier, I should have gone to a city somewhere to find a play to act in for this Christmas season. Now it appears the only theater production in Sugarplum Falls is going to give off black mold spores and potentially ruin my lungs and breath support for my

15

stage voice. No, thank you."

"Mold mitigation has already been done. They cleaned the whole thing from top to bottom, I swear. They're even scheduling the elementary school spelling bee in it. Would the school endanger the children?"

"I'm heading to the city, Archie. Hearing about the certain demise of the play is the last straw. I've made my decision."

No! Not when Owen was almost ready to give Portia his fuller attention and old-fashioned *court* her. This past year had been too crazy, as a first-year orchard manager while Dad convalesced. But a second year would be better, and he'd be able to focus on heart questions like finding a wife. He could focus on Portia, on their growing relationship.

Determining the potential of his relationship was absolutely going to be his New Year's resolution.

Like Mom had been saying for years, it was time Owen had a wife at his side, especially now that it looked like he'd be settling here in Sugarplum Falls for good. If the partner of his life could be Portia, great. Wonderful. Let the chapel bells chime.

However, Owen knew himself, and he wasn't the type to test it indefinitely through a long-distance relationship if she left.

Owen looked at Portia, but her eyes were on the floor.

"Leaving for the city!" Claire gasped, sounding as alarmed as someone who'd just been told her best friend was moving away and possibly never coming back. "You can't."

Claire's cry was heartrending, but Portia wore a resolute set to her chin. Owen had to do something, and fast. "I'll help. The play can go on."

Archie released Portia's arm and jumped toward Owen. "See, Portia? Your boyfriend will help." He turned to Owen. "What are you offering? Can you act?"

"No." Heavens, no. "I mean, before I took over management of the orchard, I ran a construction company, like Portia said. I have contacts at lumber yards and all the tools and equipment. I'll build you all new sets."

Archie tipped his head back to the ceiling, moving his lips as if uttering a prayer of thanks. Then he looked at Owen. "You're hired."

"I'm on board, too." Claire came and stood beside Owen as if in solidarity, a wall of promises meant to keep Portia in town. "Costumes? You need costumes?"

Archie threw his arms around Claire. "Of course—you have the clothing boutique."

Claire wriggled out of his grasp, and Owen relaxed his fist. Had it been clenched?

"Can you get us wholesaler discounts?" Archie bounced on his toes. "I only have the tiniest budget."

Before Claire could answer, Portia jumped in. "Claire's boutique also does tailoring. She's the best seamstress in Sugarplum Falls, and that includes all the old ladies in the quilting circles."

Claire looked at the ceiling. "If there's something unusual needed for costumes, I can probably make that happen." Pretty modest, coming from Claire, considering Portia's compliment of Claire's sewing skills had been an understatement, and even Owen knew it. "I don't want to see the Christmas play die."

Portia frowned. "Costumes and sets won't make up for the terrible play."

Not an understatement. "Lipstick on a pig," Owen said but shifted his tactics. "Portia, it's a little late to get cast in a play in a city. They probably do that in July."

Her lower lip plumped outward in an uncharacteristic pout. "Then I'll be an understudy."

"I wasn't in drama, but it probably doesn't work like that," Claire said, adding her ammo. "Aren't understudies chosen during original casting?"

"You! An understudy!" Archie went into raptures. "The thought boggles the mind. In our improved version of the town Christmas play, no one but Portia Sutherland can be the lead."

Portia lifted her eyes and made them gaze tenderly. "You'd cast me as the lead?"

The look was familiar, if not often used. Owen had been its recipient once or twice, but only over things like where to go to dinner, not in weird manipulation scenes like this one playing out before him. His skin crawled.

17

Archie drew a sharp intake of breath. "Mayor Lang would string me up for making promises prior to auditions, so we'll keep this between the four of us, all right?" He shot Owen and Claire a *take this secret to the grave for me, or else* look.

"And you're sure the script is new and improved?" Portia worked her lower lip between her teeth as if she was still on the fence about the decision.

"Could it have been worse?" Claire snuffled.

"Good point." Portia fist-punched Claire's shoulder. "Anything's better than how it's been. If you two do the costumes and sets, and with Archie's revamp of the script, maybe we can rescue the town tradition together."

"Teamwork." Archie lifted his hand for a high five. Only Claire obliged. Claire, who never left people hanging, even in high fives. Good person she was.

"It's a plan!" Portia bounced up and down. "I'll stay."

"Stay." Claire grinned. "It's the nicest four-letter word in the world."

"There's only one more thing I'll ask then." Portia stepped toward Owen. She creep-walked her fingertips up his arm, resting her hand over his bicep. "If my two favorite people in the world will also audition, then I'll do it." She smiled at him like he'd built her a castle.

Wait a second. "Me? Audition? And act in the play?"

With a violent shaking of his head *no,* Archie contradicted his body language with a tight, "That's great."

Speaking of violent shaking, Claire held her palm up. "Not me. I'll be too busy making costumes."

The argument gave Owen the perfect excuse as well—that he'd be too busy building sets—but he'd flat-out promised to do "anything" to help keep Portia around. "Aw, if I can make time to audition, you can too, Claire." Reality was, they'd probably get bit-parts, maybe even the chorus and just have to sing a few familiar carols while strolling across the stage in a couple of scenes. "It'll be fun. Do it with me. On stage."

Her face flushed redder than Santa's coat, and she mouthed the phrase *No double-entendre intended.* Now Owen's neck grew hot, and probably as red as Claire's. Blasted inside joke. He rolled his eyes at her.

18

Archie bounced glances between Claire and Owen and then frowned.

"Claire?" Portia sashayed up to Claire and clung to her arm. "Owen's right. It'll be fun if you do it with him."

Oh, geez. His mind was a septic tank sometimes.

"Fine." Claire exhaled loudly, and it blew away his wrong-thoughts. "If it makes the town's Christmas better, I'll audition. But if it's still a musical play, remember, I don't sing."

Aw, true. Claire really didn't sing. Unless you counted frogs' croaks as song.

Automatic chorus parts for him and Claire were out.

No matter. They could be walk-on villagers. Archie would keep them in the background. "Whatever it takes to save the play." Whatever it took to keep Portia in town.

"Yes!" the deep-voiced guy growl-shouted. Archie pumped Owen's hand. "Thanks. You're all right." He side-hugged Claire. "You've always been more than all right, Claire." He pressed a kiss near her temple.

A weird ping sounded in Owen's ear, and his spine stiffened. Was that guy hitting on Claire? He'd hugged her with enthusiasm a minute ago. No. Not a good match. Owen would have to step in if it continued. That guy wasn't on Claire's level.

Grinning, Archie left, slamming the front door.

Portia twirled twice before thrusting herself into Owen's arms. "Isn't it wonderful?" Her kiss was supple against his neck. He'd have a dark red stain there later for the family to quirk an eyebrow at. "We're saving the play. Together."

"Do you really think it was necessary?" Owen ran his hands down her arms.

"I'm with Owen." Claire pulled the tablecloth off and shook it over the sink. "Everyone comes to the play no matter what. It's in the Sugarplum Falls residents' contract."

Not true, but might as well be.

"And what was with the flirting with the director?" Owen asked before he could stop himself. "You've played Caroline the last three years, and there'd

19

probably be some kind of uprising in the town if you didn't get it."

"They do like me." She batted her lashes and did her Sally Field at the Oscars impression. "They really like me."

"You're a goof." Claire whipped her with the dishtowel, and Portia lunged for it. They chased around the kitchen like they were twelve years old, until Portia had snapped the towel at Claire twice.

Then she sat on the counter. "I shouldn't be so mean to him. Really, he's not a bad guy simply because we used to date and he dumped me the summer after high school before college."

"You left town." Claire started the hot water running again.

There was probably more to that history, Archie's side of things. Plus a few details Portia obviously wasn't saying. Her acting skills were good, but not that good.

In moments like these, when Portia lost some of her shine, that gave Owen pause. No doubt, she was a great girlfriend. Vibrant, attentive, patient with his immersion in his business—in ways few women would be. Plus, she'd charmed his entire family. Breaking up with her over something small would be ridiculous.

But he did pause. And then vacillated.

As a business owner, Owen had learned to take the whole situation into consideration, to weigh pros and cons, costs and benefits. Play the long game. He'd invested a full year into dating Portia, but not a full year's worth of effort. He hadn't given her a real chance yet.

If he were to let her go, he'd spend the rest of his life wondering.

Saving the play and keeping Portia around was the right thing to do, even if it meant standing on a stage to sing, swinging a hammer to build sets for the theater, or having to wear a top-hat from the Victorian era.

Plus, he'd be helping Claire, too. Look at all she'd done to find new friends tonight. Keeping Portia for Claire's sake mattered too.

Chapter 3

Claire

With a sweep of her hand, she brushed crumbs off her sweater. Claire set down her leftover turkey sandwich—her third this week already, since her big turkey-bake over the weekend. She'd be eating them for weeks to come, too, thanks to the nonexistent crowd she'd cooked for.

Enough lunch. Back to sewing. The back room of Apple Blossom Boutique was piled high with bolts of fabric, patterns both cut and uncut, and a jumble of notions that might have fallen straight out of Dickensian times.

Thirteen blouses, all with buttons up the front and up the sleeves. Unlucky thirteen.

Thirteen was the number of Claire's Originals dress designs she'd created and sewn sale-ready batches for—but had never taken out of the stock room and put on the shelves.

Stupid, paralyzing fear.

"Claire, Claire, Claire! These are going to be incredible." Lulu held up a set of Victorian dress patterns like a fan. They'd been overnight-shipped after Claire and Archie had consulted on what was needed. Earlier this week, Claire had nearly cleared Threads–n–Things out of cotton, calico, and superfine fabric.

"Presser-foot to the metal."

"Are you going to sew them all yourself? I'd offer to help, but I'm much more the ready-to-wear type." Lulu's long-bygone glory days of *almost* becoming a fashion model flashed across her face. That dream had been dashed by two things: Lulu's short stature and her too-bright smile even when her face rested. Fashion models needed resting-frown-faces, not barely contained mirth. "But, I can order stuff. Anything you need."

Claire's business partner and half owner of Apple Blossom Boutique was best at moral support, but good at many things, especially dealing with customers when Claire retreated to her mending and tailoring pile in the back.

"Could you jump online and request these?" She handed Lulu a list, complete with pictures of all the costume pieces Claire and Archie had agreed on. "Mayor Lang upped our budget when I showed her the numbers of what it would really cost to replace everything destroyed in the flood."

Lulu nodded. "How's she going to pay for it? That couldn't be in the town budget."

"Charge for tickets to the play."

"Honestly?" Lulu's hand covered her mouth for a second. "She thinks anyone will *pay* to watch that show? When it's always been free in the past, and when everyone's already seen it every Christmas of their lives? What's she thinking?"

"Who knows?" Not Claire's problem—unless Archie didn't come through with reimbursement. "But, hey. Let's also make sure we have our own store inventory set. The rush of moms who want matching mother-daughter dresses usually starts right about now." Once the Sugarplum Falls moms had been to the first December Sunday in church, they all seemed to feel a sudden nostalgic tug for matching mommy-daughter dresses. "Anything else?"

"Don't forget the little boys' suit jackets. Gotta have those. Get the holiday church dress-up days covered." Lulu clicked her heels together.

"Thanks."

"One year," Lulu smiled, "I got matching suit jackets for Eugene and our son. Ah, times gone by." Their son was an accountant now, expecting a son of his own. "They looked like Little Lord Fauntleroy and Big Lord Fauntleroy. They didn't let me shop for them after that."

Their eyes met and they did a simultaneous cringe.

"Don't worry about me and the shop. You should get started on that stackola of work." Lulu headed toward the shop floor, and Claire followed. "Or you'll never have those costumes done in time for opening night."

No lie. Frankly, there was no way she could do costumes *and* try out for the play. Just running the shop was more than a full-time job. Sewing all new costumes for the play, too? Croaksville on her sleep schedule.

"Correct me if I'm wrong, but you're burning the candle at both ends."

"Not wrong."

"I meant to say, you're sure doing a lot for Portia." Lulu shifted her pile of sweaters higher on her hip. "I love the girl as much as the next person, but isn't she kind of a diva? Why are you letting her do this to you?"

No one could understand if they hadn't known the decade-long dynamic between Claire and Portia. "She's been a great friend to me."

"Great friends don't chain their friends to sewing machines."

No, but they did do stuff like make sure Claire was never left out. Back in high school, whenever Portia had been asked on a date, she'd only say yes on the condition that her guy got a pal to double with them and include Claire. She never acted like doing so hindered her good times, either. And Portia carried the conversation on those dates so that Claire could just smile and enjoy whatever activity they were doing.

Or the fact that when Apple Blossom Boutique opened, Portia had willingly headed up all the interaction with the press, and Claire had been able to smile from the sidelines. Portia loved the spotlight, and Claire loved being outside of it.

But beyond those times, when Mom remarried and Claire had had a lot of feelings about Eddy, Portia had been the one to listen.

On the surface, and to others, Portia might not seem like a bosom friend—as Anne of Green Gables might say—but Claire knew her better than anyone and had needed her for years.

Losing her to the call of the stage was just not thinkable.

"Trust me, our friendship isn't one-sided." Claire picked through the patterns, deciding where to go next. Besides, she loved being at her sewing

23

machine.

"Oh, by the way. I never thought to ask. How did your supper club thing go?" Lulu lingered at the doorway of the office. "I guess Owen came?"

"Sure, he was there." Why ask about him? "Portia, Owen, and then Archie Holdaway."

"Of course." Lulu fluffed her blonde-to-hide-the-gray hair and headed out.

What was that about? Whatever. No time to chat or think. Sew, just sew.

At least sewing all the blouses, skirts, and vests for the play was *something new* Claire could report to Mom. And they'd be seen on the stage. They weren't her own designs, so it wasn't exactly meeting Mom's requirement, but progress was progress, right?

Claire put her head down and spread out her patterns to start cutting and pinning and cutting and pinning. Lulu could handle the front of the store. This task would take all afternoon, and beyond.

Sometime later, the front door jingled a few times, always with shoppers, until—

"Is Claire in?" a gravel-laced bass voice asked.

"Archie!" Lulu's voice carried through the store. "I heard you'd taken that teaching job at the high school. Good to see you back again. How are your folks?"

"They're fine. Can I see Claire?"

Archie must have been in a hurry. Who could blame him? The play was a lot of pressure.

"Sure. Just a sec." Lulu's footsteps approached on the wood floors of Apple Blossom Boutique.

Claire should've gotten up and gone out to greet him, but she had two more pins to place, and the pattern's tissue paper might slide if she bumped it wrong by moving, and—

The bells jingled again. "Oh, Archie! There you are." A different woman's voice filled the whole room—the mayor. "I'm so glad I could run into you. We have *so* much to discuss about the town Christmas play."

"Oh, hi, Mayor Lang." Archie didn't mask his lack of enthusiasm. "Don't

24

worry, I'm on task this very minute."

Whew, the mayor had just bought her some time. Sure, Claire felt bad eavesdropping, but until she got these pinned, she had no choice. To keep the fabric from being spoiled, she had to delay—and overhear.

"The play really should have a title, don't you think? It's so generic, even after all these years." Mayor Lang's laugh was like the Wicked Witch of the West's, more of a cackle than a laugh. "But I'll put you on that task. You're the director."

"Uh-huh." Archie sounded unconvinced of his own authority, and the next tidbit from Mayor Lang likely drove that doubt home.

"Now, the reason I tracked you down—casting." Mayor Lang's voice lowered, but it still carried through the rafters to Claire's sewing room as clear as through a megaphone. "With the rewrites, you know how important it is to me that Portia Sutherland not be cast as Caroline this year."

What? Portia not star in the town Christmas play? What kind of a holiday-bashing Scrooge-fest was going on in Mayor Lang's mind? Claire surged to her feet to go in and argue, but she'd accidentally sewed her shirt sleeve to the skirt attached to the sewing machine.

I'm stuck!

"Hey?" She yanked at her blouse. The conversation out there had to be stopped! Normally, Claire never would take on the task, but this was an emergency. "Hey?" she called but without response. "Guys?"

How tacky would it be to holler her disapproval—and signal that she'd been eavesdropping? Not as tacky as taking off her shirt and racing out there to disagree. She'd go pretty far to defend a friend—but toplessness?

The mayor might be too shocked to argue …

Claire bent over her shirt and began unpicking with the seam-ripper as fast as possible.

"I've already thought it through, Mayor. I've got my casting plans for leads in place."

"Then we're of the same mind?"

"Like you said, I'm the director."

Good for Archie, standing up for his creative autonomy! Or, was he agreeing? Oh, there was no way to tell without reading the clues on Archie's not-so-poker face. He had a poker voice, instead. Which was not helpful in this moment.

"I'm counting on you, Archie Holdaway. I want this year to be the best ever for the town Christmas play." A little stomp of a boot sounded through the air. "And get on renaming it, would you?"

"On it," he said. "Now, I need to get to the theater to prepare paperwork for auditions, Mayor. If you'll excuse me."

The door bell jingled an exit, just as the last stitch came loose. Claire flew from her office to the front of the store. No one remained but Lulu.

"Did you get an earful of that?" Claire breathed. "What in the actual heck?"

Lulu gave a sad shake of her head. "Portia Sutherland is going to need some serious emotional support if she doesn't get the part of Caroline."

"Do you really think Archie Holdaway would kowtow to the mayor's demands like that?"

"The mayor gets what she wants."

"But—" But Archie still cared about Portia. Or at least he'd seemed to the other night at Claire's failed Christmas supper. "Why would he hurt her like that?"

"Revenge?"

Oh. *Oh.* It was true that Portia had chosen going to the coast to study dramatic arts over going off to college with Archie, but that was a long time ago. And Archie had been the dumper, not the dump-ee.

Then again, revenge was a dish best served cold. This would be icebox cold, after so many years, but still—Archie could be scheming.

"Should I warn her?" Claire was torn. Anyone in this situation, dramatic personality or not, might shoot the messenger and get upset with Claire instead of at Mayor Lang or at Archie. "She deserves to know what's coming."

"And make Portia hate the mayor forevermore, on the outside chance that Archie will cave to her pressure?" Lulu scrunched up her lips.

Good point. Archie really didn't seem like the revenge type. Plus, Claire was armed with knowledge that Mayor Lang didn't possess: at the Supper of

26

Lameness, Portia had extracted from Archie a half-promise he'd cast her as lead.

Moreover, Archie maintained an obvious spark of interest in Portia. Not cool, especially not for Owen. Maybe if Owen could up their relationship to the next level, Archie would get the hint.

Owen and Portia. Portia and Owen. He was so good for her. Any girl would be lucky to have Owen as a boyfriend. *And I love Portia. I want her to have the best.*

"Fine. You're correct about one big thing, no matter what." Claire examined the little needle pricks in her shirt's sleeve. "That if casting ends up a surprise, Portia will need extra emotional support."

She might even pack her bags and leave.

And take with her all my memories. Every brave thing Claire had ever done—from karaoke to writing holiday letters to the troops, from painting storefront windows during homecoming week to learning to ski at Frosty Ridge Lodge—she'd done with Portia.

Without Portia, Claire might never have been brave. Without her, she might never be brave again.

Portia had been there for Claire. It was time for Claire to be there for Portia.

I guess I have to audition for the town Christmas play.

Oh, brother. But being there on site to offer constant reassurance was the best way to keep Portia's spirits up—and her physical person here in Sugarplum Falls. Claire glanced at the clock. Auditions were slated to begin in an hour.

I can't believe I'm doing this.

27

Chapter 4

Owen

Kneeling over three successive four-by-eight pieces of plywood, Owen used his electric drill to screw hinges on the backs of what would eventually become the set for the outdoor winter scene. Handles on the backs of the pieces were next. Then felt would be applied to the bottoms for easy sliding.

Foldable set pieces were Owen's creative contribution to the cause. Portia, as the star, might not appreciate the innovation, since she wouldn't be the one hauling them onstage and off, but the crew would.

Anything to make the play more of a success was Owen's goal.

"Hey, Owen. Cool. You're already hard at work." Up walked Archie. "You got a second? I need to let you know about a few things that will have to change the sets, due to the script rewrite."

Owen stood up and shook Archie's hand. The guy looked a lot less crazed today than he had at Claire's place. Maybe Owen should give him the benefit of the doubt. "What kinds of changes?"

"To the script? A lot. To the sets, not as many. I'll need replicas of all the old familiar sets, plus a few more that look like this." Archie pulled a folded piece of paper from his suit-coat pocket. It contained diagrams of a small tower-like structure, almost like a Juliet balcony, decorated with harps and clouds. "It'll be the angel's stand."

There was an angel in the story? Must be part of the rewrite. "Does it need to be on wheels?"

"If you think that would make it easier to move, sure. Good idea." Archie looked relieved. "Thanks, man. This play was completely in the ditch after that flood last month. I thought I was going to have to tell the mayor we weren't doing it. Not that many people would mind. Except maybe Portia."

"I've got her back." In spite of having to simultaneously have Archie's back.

"I'll make it up to you somehow." Archie left the drawings with Owen. "If we stick together like this, she'll be really pleased." A gleam lit Archie's eye.

Owen's neck bunched up again. Was the *she* in his sentence a reference to Mayor Lang or to Portia? The other night, Archie had certainly seemed dedicated to earning Owen's girlfriend's attention. Hmmm. Too bad there was no other venue for Portia to get her acting fix here in town—*away* from Archie Holdaway.

Of course, rumor had it that actresses and actors usually ended up hating the directors, so maybe Archie would mess up and make Portia hate him sooner rather than later. That'd be good.

Out in the theater, the seats slowly filled with Sugarplum Falls citizens. Audition time.

Owen finished up the set piece he was working on, then dragged it backstage and went to find Portia. Surely, she was in the house somewhere. Instead, he came across Claire first.

"You made it." He sat down beside her. "Are you here to audition?" Unexpected, but not unwelcome.

She nodded. "You, too?"

"Portia can be very persuasive." Which may or may not have sounded like a double-entendre. He sneaked a glance at Claire. She hadn't picked up on it. What was it about Claire that made him resurrect their old double-entendre joke? "Are you reciting something, or singing, or what? Monologue?"

"I'll probably just read from whatever script Archie has lying up on the stage for us newbies and less hard-core types."

29

"That description fits me precisely." Owen had briefly considered attempting to piece together the fragments of his *Hamlet* monologue he'd memorized in high school, but that could go south fast. "I'll follow your lead."

"You'll dazzle them." Claire pushed against his shoulder with hers. These seats were sure narrow. Her shoulder still rested against his. "Portia here yet?"

"She likes to make an entrance." Owen didn't move his shoulder. Somehow Claire's arm comforted his nerves. "Let it be noted: acting is way outside my comfort zone."

Claire chuckled. "I'm hoping I'll get on the stage and be the most forgettable thing Archie's ever seen, and he can put me at the back of the pack of Christmas carolers that only come on for a single scene."

Owen took a surreptitious glance at Claire. Instead of her usual, comfy after-work clothes that he saw her in when the three of them hung out, she was dressed like a woman who owned a high-end clothing store. In her dark green silk top and cream slacks that accentuated her long legs, set off by the gold filigree necklaces and earrings matched her gold high-heeled shoes, Archie would notice. He'd have to be dead not to.

Owen's protective shields went up. Even if Archie was less of an irritant today than he'd been when they first met at dinner, something about him taking notice of Claire didn't sit right with Owen.

The fact was, Claire deserved someone stellar—someone like Nicholas, the lead character from the town Christmas play. For all the shortcomings of the cheesy story, the hero was probably the one element that kept people coming back year after year. He was kind, sacrificing, and his final lines gave everyone a feel-good holiday moment.

Yeah, Claire deserved a Nicholas for sure.

As their names were called, a few dozen teens and adults filed across the stage, each offering their prepared lines. Some could project to the back of the house, others not.

Where was Portia? Owen twisted in his seat. No sign of her.

Making an entrance or not, Portia had better make her appearance in time to audition. If there was one thing certain, Archie couldn't offer her the lead if she didn't even show up to try out.

"It's a good thing you're auditioning, too." Claire's scent wafted over him. It was more vanilla than usual. Smelled good. "I think Portia is going to need both of us to get through this production." Her voice had a slight edge.

"Maybe, but then again, Portia's an adult. She's been in enough theater productions by now she should be able to handle script changes or dramatic pressure."

"Uh-huh." Claire didn't sound so sure.

"Oh, do you want to see something?" He pulled out the set design change. "There's going to be this tower thing added to the set design." More pages came out with the paper from Archie, and they fell across his lap.

"What's that?"

He gathered them up. "Just a few scrawls of my own." He unfolded the sketch of the angel tower, but Claire seemed more intrigued by the designs Owen had drawn.

"Can I take a look? This one is really good. Check out how innovative that folding piece is! The crew will love you. Did you draw the decoration as well?"

He had. "I'm no artist."

"Beg to differ." She handed them back to Owen. "Have you shown these to Archie yet?"

"There's enough other pressure on the dude today, so not yet," he said, just as Archie rushed up the aisle to their seats.

"Is she here? I haven't seen her yet. Did she head to the ladies' room or something?" Wild-eyed, Archie's gaze darted around the house. "I'm going to be in deep trouble if she doesn't show up."

"You won't have a leading lady," Claire said flatly. "No one to play Caroline."

Archie froze and then lowered his gaze to Claire. "That's right." He pushed his mouth to the side of his face. "If you hear from her, please let me know."

Weird. The guy was flat-out weird.

They politely listened to another slew of auditions as the director summoned wannabe actors in succession, but still no Portia. Some were pretty good, including Donny and Marie Gatwick, brother and sister dynamos. They were almost as sparkly as the original Osmond brother-sister duo. They should get leading parts, if not leads—except for the kiss at the end part.

Ew.

After a while, everyone else in the house had been up, other than Claire and Owen, who grew sicker by the minute. Soon enough, the gong struck.

"Owen Kingston, Claire Sutherland." Archie called them to the stage. "You're up."

Owen looked to Claire. "Here goes nothing."

"Nothing's right. Nothing memorable."

She was funny. "Here." Owen held her hand to assist as she ascended the stairs stage right in those heels, then he jogged up the steps and met her center stage. They each read from the scripts the familiar words of the time-worn play.

"Oh, Nicholas. It's beautiful," Claire read in a Caroline voice, but better than he would have expected. It was sincere, full of feminine warmth. She looked up at him with the same love Caroline should have for Nicholas after all he's done for her in the story. "You did this all for me?"

"I hope you don't mind the imperfections." Owen knew his delivery was flat. He'd better step it up for Portia's sake, in case she showed up at the theater now and saw him phoning it in. "I hope you know that no matter what, it's infused with both love and the Christmas Spirit."

"It's the most beautiful nativity scene anyone ever built in a sickroom, Nicholas."

The cheese was so thick it could be cut with a knife, but a little sigh erupted from somewhere down in the first few rows, followed by, *"It's such a sweet story. I love it."*

Oh, brother. But he had to end with a flourish, just in case.

Owen finished up his lines. "You just get better, Caroline. That is the only Christmas present I'm asking for this year." He took Claire in his arms and kissed her forehead. She was supple and smelled even more like vanilla candles up close. "Your love is the best gift I could imagine."

Claire looked up at him, still perched in his arms. Her hands were placed

32

flat against his chest, and a longing simmered in her gaze. Suddenly Owen found himself caught in the moment, in her stare. A little harp's string plucked at the back of his chest, the resonance of which radiated outward through his body, creating a ringing in his ears.

Applause disrupted his thoughts. Or lack of them.

Claire tugged away, and Owen relaxed his hold on her. They exited stage-left.

Whoa, Claire's acting might give Portia a run for her money.

"Thanks, Claire and Owen." Archie stood from his place in the center of the theater. "Anyone else? Anyone? Please?"

"I'm here!" Portia floated down the aisle in full holiday regalia, all smiles and sequins. "Are you ready for me, darling?"

"Owen, you stay up there with her, please?" Archie directed.

"Oh, Archie, but I've prepared a monologue. Don't you know me better than that?"

"Perfect." Archie allowed it, and Owen and Claire returned to where they'd been sitting.

"Whew. Glad that's over," she said. "Could you feel me shaking up there?"

Owen could feel something from Claire, but it hadn't been shaking. "You seemed pretty confident to me."

"You're just being kind."

Kind? *Kind* of swept up in the moment, more like. "You may have missed your calling."

"My calling is with the needle and thread, trust me."

Up on the stage, Portia performed a combination of speaking, singing, and choreography that would wow any director from here to Broadway. It displayed a huge range of emotion, ending with her hands clutched at her chest, tears welling, and her lower lip quivering.

"Wonderful, Portia." Archie launched the applause himself. "Touching. Deeply touching."

Someone a few rows behind where Claire and Owen sat whispered, "That's why she always gets the Caroline role. She's amazing."

33

No arguments from Owen. Portia commanded every iota of attention in the room. She had charm, vibrancy—an energy that you'd have to be comatose to ignore. She finished her audition with a sweep of her long skirt and a darling curtsey that didn't really fit her severe dark haircut or her intense eyes, but which put her breadth of skills on display.

She was, indeed, amazing.

"Thank you, everyone." Archie joined Portia on the stage, placed an arm around her waist, and whispered something in her ear.

Owen bristled, Portia colored, but Archie addressed the room. "A huge thank you to everyone who tried out. If you would like to stay around, I'll have the casting lists posted within the hour. Note—my decisions are final. As a reminder for those who haven't worked professionally in the past, in theater the protocol is that actors don't argue with or complain about casting decisions. If you happened to get a less-desirable role, dropping out is bad form. Directors note it, and word gets around in acting and directing circles. So, I recommend accepting your assigned part with grace and gratitude. Remember, there are no small parts, only small actors."

Owen huffed and muttered, "What does that saying even mean?"

Claire simultaneously muttered, "What does that even mean?" She turned her head and their eyes met. She placed a hand in front of her mouth to cover her smile. "You, too?"

Owen nodded. "At least Archie knows I'm more than happy with the world's tiniest role, whether or not I'm a small actor." Beside Claire, he'd felt pretty huge up there. Protective. Possessive.

Weird.

"Me, too." Claire stood up. "The smaller the better. Invisible would be best. Or not even in the cast. I've got enough to do and more with the costumes alone."

"So true. You're doing a lot for this. Thank you." Owen really owed her for helping keep Portia in town. Somehow he'd have to pay her back. Since she said she was looking for friends to spend time with, maybe he could find Claire someone great, a Nicholas. There were a lot of Kingston men he could tap for that. Why hadn't he considered setting Claire up with one of them before now?

34

"Oh, Owen!" Portia hurtled toward him. "I caught the tail-end of your audition. You were divine!" She sank against his torso, wrapping her arms around his waist. "I'm exhausted from my tryout. Do you all want to go eat while we wait for casting decisions?"

"Wait for the list?" Claire said. "Could we just check it tomorrow?"

"Claire has a lot of sewing to do." Owen spoke up to defend Claire's time. "You could text her with the results." And text him while Portia was at it. Owen had a gargantuan orchard to tend.

"Text her!" Portia gasped, as if Owen had just suggested canceling Santa this year. "Not a chance. I've changed my mind about dinner. Instead, we're going to sit here like a happy trio of friends and wait for our fate to be decreed. Although, I have a strong feeling it's going to go our way." She grinned like the Cheshire Cat. "Don't you?"

Uh-huh. At least in Portia's case, it was more or less guaranteed, based on the little whisper Archie had dropped in Portia's ear on stage.

Inappropriate.

Out in the lobby, they found a grouping of sofas and sat down as other would-be actors filled the foyer. The theater's signature plush blue carpet had been torn out and replaced with deep red, likely post-flood. New drapes hung from the windows, and touches of gold paint had been added everywhere. It looked pretty good. Now, if only there were going to be a production to match the upgrade.

Couldn't the town just put on a production of *A Christmas Carol* instead? No one would mind watching that year after year.

"I'm so sorry I missed your audition, Claire. But I did see you up there with Owen. With those heels on, you're the exact right height to be paired onstage. Not likely, but you're so cute together." She coughed and gave a confident smile. "We're going to have so much fun doing this play together!"

Owen glanced at Claire, whose face had grown pink. Owen's was warm, too. Yeah, it was definitely unsettling to hear things like *you and my best friend make a cute couple* coming from his own girlfriend.

"The thing I'm most anxious about is getting back to Mt. Fabric-us." Claire reached for her coat. "Seriously, text me? It could be hours."

That kid Declan who seemed to be everywhere in town, hurried through the lobby. "Casting list is up. Casting list is up. It's on the dressing room door backstage." He must be acting as Archie's go-fer now.

"Casting list!" Portia gasped. Claire looked sick, even scared.

A stampede formed.

"Portia, wait. It's—" Claire reached for her, but caught air. Portia took the lead as the mob hustled down the aisles and then through to the backstage area.

Owen hung back with Claire. "I guess we're the only ones not too anxious to find out our parts." He leaned against the wall at the back of the theater's seating. "Unless you are?"

"I'm anxious all right." Claire glanced at the madding crowd, when a shriek pierced the air that practically reversed the blood's flow in Owen's arteries.

Portia.

"Archie Holdaway! Who on earth do you think you are?"

Chapter 5

Claire

Claire might as well have been standing on the tracks of an oncoming train. Collision was imminent.

Portia charged up the aisle to where Owen and Claire stood at the back of the theater—with Archie hot on her heels in full-on simpering mode.

I should have warned her. I could have prevented this meltdown.

"Claire Downing!"

"Me?"

"I mean, maybe you didn't do it on purpose, but—but the Caroline part was supposed to be mine. I thought it was understood. And now, you—"

Archie grabbed her arm. "Portia, slow down and listen." Archie hopped from foot to foot. Up on the stage, dozens of pairs of eyes peered uncomfortably at the four of them. "I had a very good reason."

"A good reason to give *my* role to *her?*" She swooped her arm at Claire.

"To whom?" Claire touched her throat. "Not me. No."

If Portia had been a pinball machine, her eyes would have been flashing *Tilt! Tilt! Tilt!* She held up a finger at Archie, but Owen stepped in.

"Ho, ho, hold up, Portia."

Archie looked like he'd just been force-fed stale fruitcake and was spluttering out the dry crumbs.

"Obviously there's been a mistake." Owen took Portia's hand, and she visibly relaxed. Owen was so good for her.

"Right?" Her eyes flashed at Archie again.

"Obviously," Claire muttered. "When something gets mistyped, people just need to take a deep breath, all right?" Just once before, Claire had been on the receiving end of one of Portia's tirades, but this one put the previous rant to shame. "Let the guy explain that he made a clerical error, okay?" She turned to Archie. "It's a simple mistake, of course. Right, Archie? Right?"

Archie dug the white rubber tips of his Converse shoes into the carpet. "Portia, it's not what you think right now."

Did that mean—? Claire's heart clenched. Archie had caved to Mayor Lang's pressure! But why *me*?

Claire's eye began to twitch. Her years-long friendship with Portia could potentially crash on the casting rocks over something this huge.

"Explain." Owen pushed Portia behind him and loomed over Archie, hands on hips, fixing a steely glare on the guy. "Right now. And I don't want to hear any guff about *don't question the casting director's decisions*. You and I and all of us know that's not what's going on here."

Archie Holdaway looked like a little kid, cowering under Owen's bulk. In all Claire's days of knowing Archie, he'd always been pretty cool. Confident. Together. Right now, all of that vanished, as he shrank beneath all their glares.

Claire joined the pressure-fest. "Archie, you need to explain to Portia what's going on." If not, Claire planned to reveal him for the sell-out he was. "I know you're dealing with a lot of external demands." Would he catch her drift?

From behind Owen, Portia kept jumping to peer over his shoulder at Archie with murder in her eyes. "You *know* I can't quit a play. You *know* I can't question casting."

Other than with shrieks to fill the theater, apparently.

"Portia, please." Archie looked green around the gills.

"Show me the list." Owen stood firm until Archie pulled out a second copy from his stack of papers on his clipboard. "Caroline, Claire Downing." Owen shot Claire a stunned look that made her nearly topple off her high-heeled shoes.

This wasn't happening. Claire couldn't star in a play!

"Evangeline, Portia Sutherland." Owen frowned. "We've all seen this play enough to know that Evangeline is not a character in the story."

"It is! She is!" Archie looked ready to pop. "Come on, guys. I told you. I promised to give Portia the leading role. It's exactly what I said I'd do."

A low growl emanated from Portia's direction, slowly growing to a shout. "Everyone knows Caroline is the leading role!" Tears formed, possibly real tears. "Oh, Owen. It's not fair."

Staring patrons lined up on the stage.

"We should take this discussion outside," Claire whispered to Owen.

Owen hustled the four of them out into the narrow street that hosted the red-door entrance to Kingston Theater. A bicycle leaned up against the brick wall, probably Declan's.

The crisp air smelled like wood stoves. Claire rubbed her arms against the cold, as they stood in a circle, their breaths turning to vapor under the streetlamp's light. They needed to resolve this before frostbite set in.

"Archie, you'd better start talking." Claire wasn't usually cross with people, but it had been a long day. A series of them.

"I told you, there was a rewrite to the script."

"And now Caroline has been revamped?" Portia's voice was tight and high-pitched. "There's a different heroine altogether?"

"No, no." Finally, the faucet untwisted and Archie's explanation flowed forth. "Evangeline is the angel. She's the narrator of the whole story. Caroline and Nicholas are still the lead *humans*, but Evangeline is the main storyteller. She is the one the audience connects with. She's the guide for their experience in the production, and she has twice the number of lines as everyone else put together."

Portia sniffled and swatted at her eyes. "The character is an angel?"

"It's fitting, don't you think?" Were those stars in Archie's eyes? Oh, brother.

Portia's eye mists lifted. "There hasn't been an angel in the play before. What about costume design?"

From Archie's stack attached to the clipboard he pulled a sheet of paper. "This is a rough of the design I had in mind." He turned to Claire. "I came by to drop it off for you today, but I got interrupted. Do you think you can make this?"

Another costume? On top of all the costumes she was already in charge of—plus learning all the lines for the play in the role of Caroline? "It's beautiful. I'm happy to do this." Sort of. *If you'll let me change roles in the play.* "What part did Owen get?" She had to change the subject before she got roped into yet another huge, time-sucking vortex.

Portia flew to Owen's side. "You're going to be a townsperson. Just like you wanted."

Lucky dog. Claire shot him a look of pure jealousy, and he feigned being wounded by it.

Then, the bomb dropped. Kapow! And not a candy bomb.

"Fletch Fletcher is going to play Nicholas," Portia said, as if she weren't talking about the worst fate in the world for Claire.

Fletcher the Lecher? Alarm bells rang. No consummate actress, Claire didn't mask her concern.

Neither did Owen. "Archie. You didn't." If Claire had ever seen a deeper frown on Owen's face, she couldn't remember one. "You'd better amend that list. Pronto."

"No other men auditioned fitting Nicholas's description. And for the record, all three of you are crossing the clearly drawn line of *no questioning the casting director's decisions* here."

"We should set an example." A suddenly subservient Portia placed a hand on Owen's chest. "For the other cast members. Besides, Fletch will know how to dial up the on-stage chemistry with Claire."

Heavenly days. Claire reached for Declan's bicycle handle to steady herself. The town Christmas play ended with a kiss! And she was going to be forced to hide a gag reflex. On stage. With Fletch, who considered cologne a substitute for hygiene and every woman a target for his unwelcome advances.

"This will be so good for you, Claire." Portia launched at her and pulled Claire into a huge hug. "You said you wanted to try something new. It's been so long since you kissed anyone, this is a perfect *new* experience. Your mom will be so proud. She might even come and watch it. Bring her new husband and everything."

"Portia." Claire nodded toward Archie. "We're not just you and me here."

"Portia." Owen shushed her, even though Owen pretty much knew all of that already—except maybe the ages-since-kissed part, and he could have guessed that anyway. "Archie is listening."

"He's one of us, hon." Portia linked her arms with both Owen and Archie. Claire drew her neck back in shock.

The theater's front door banged open, and—great. Fletch burst around the corner and out into the narrow street. Snow flurried up around his ankles as he stalked, panther-like, toward Claire.

"There you are, my leading lady." A devilish hunger lit his eye, and he continued toward them, his eyes trained on her, his latest prey. "When I auditioned, I hoped, but I didn't dare hope *this* high." He swept her into his arms and aimed a kiss for her mouth.

She turned her head just in time, and he planted it on her cheek instead. Gross. There was tongue, like an untrained puppy.

"Playing hard to get. I like it. Well, I say we get in a lot of after-hours rehearsal time at my place, perfecting our chemistry off-stage so that it will transfer well and give the viewing public their money's worth. When Archie Holdaway told me this was going to be the best year for the town Christmas play ever, I knew I had to do my part to help."

Fletch's breath smelled like someone had generously spiked his eggnog and he'd swilled way too many quarts of it since dinner. Claire pushed her way out of his arms. "Fletch, that's not how it's going to be."

"Yeah." Owen stepped over and laid a hand on Fletch's shoulder, and it looked like he pushed it down. Hard. "Absolutely not."

"And who do you think *you* are, *townsperson*? Not the leading man. So, I don't see you have any authority telling the star of the play what he can or can't do with the leading lady." Fletch yanked his shoulder out from beneath Owen's grip and leaned right into his face. He poked Owen in the chest repeatedly. "You've got your girlfriend. Isn't one woman enough? You

Kingston men are all the same. You expect all the women to fall for you, but I'm here to prove you wrong tonight. My Caroline and I are getting cozy on and off stage. And you can't stop us."

He let out a Tarzan yell and pounded his chest. The yodel echoed up through the high walls of the alley.

Claire backed away, leaning up against the wall of the theater and burying her face in the crook of her elbow. How had she allowed herself to get into this situation? She had to quit. But she couldn't quit. She needed Fletch to quit. But there was no way that would happen.

Suddenly, all went silent. She peeked an eye over her arm.

Fletch was on the ground, his eyes closed.

Portia stepped gingerly toward him. "Fletch? Buddy, you okay?" She crouched beside the inert body. "Should we call an ambulance?"

"On it." Owen already had his phone out.

Archie looked stricken. "Should I take his pulse?"

"I will." Claire hustled over and moved the guy's scarf down. She felt the side of his neck. "He's breathing." Not dead. Whew.

"I think he hit his head when he went down."

O, the perils of demon rum-eggnog. Claire squinted to summon courage. Then she turned to Archie. "Despite my oath to not interfere with your casting decisions, Fletch isn't a good choice for Nicholas." Setting aside the facts that he had none of the character's morals and he'd already sexually harassed Claire in the first thirty seconds, there was a bigger reason. "Archie, this is a family play. Meaning, you have kids of all ages in the cast. You can't have this"—she indicated the inert mass—"person as Nicholas. The kids are watching him and will look up to him and follow what he does."

"You're probably right." Archie rubbed the side of his head. "In case you didn't notice, though, there was a glaring lack of men at auditions. I didn't have a lot to choose from."

True. In the entire room of wannabe actors, there'd been barely a handful of adult males. Obviously, the script of the town Christmas play itself was a factor.

"You could rewrite it to have teenagers as the stars," Claire offered.

42

"There were a few teenage boys in there." *Just so long as Claire didn't have to star opposite one of them and incur creeped-out glares from the town.* "I'd gladly step down from Caroline's role. Could Portia play both the angel and Caroline?"

"You'd do that?" Portia lit up.

"Too many simultaneous on-stage scenes. All of them, in fact."

Portia's face scrunched. So did Claire's. There was no way out, at least not for Claire. Maybe she should take up rum-eggnog and disqualify herself, too.

An ambulance's siren cut the night air, and Archie groaned. "The teen thing would be a good idea, but I've already put too much time into the rewrite, and it takes even more time to get the city council to approve it. Believe me when I say we don't have time to go through that, considering we're already almost in December. Plus, I'd have to redo all casting, and auditions, and ... no. Unless Fletch can pull himself together, I think I'll have to cancel the play this year."

Portia gasped. "But all of Owen's sets! And Claire's gorgeous costumes!" She tugged at her skirts, probably imagining the Evangeline angel costume.

"Maybe next year." Archie looked glum, but that made Portia look even glummer.

"I should have gone to the city." Portia looked positively devastated. "The town play will die, Archie. No one will be able to resuscitate it if we cancel it even once."

"You can still find an acting gig, Portia." Archie touched her arm lightly. "It's late in the season, but I'm sure there's something somewhere."

Somewhere else, he meant.

No. There had to be a solution here. *One that doesn't involve my kissing Fletcher the Lecher.* Claire racked her brain.

The ambulance pulled up, and three EMTs surrounded Fletch, taking his vitals, loading him onto a stretcher, taking statements from Claire, Portia, and Owen.

Once loaded into the ambulance, Fletch started moaning. "Where am I? Where's my leading lady? I want her. She's mine."

Claire cringed. It was getting really cold outside now. Her stomach muscles quaked.

"So, you say he yodeled and then collapsed?" an EMT asked, taking notes on a tablet. "Sounds about like what they said happened right before he busted out of rehab this morning. We've been trying to hunt him down ever since. He still has three weeks left on in-patient status. Seems his family's wish that he be ankle-tagged is going to come true."

Ankle-tagged! Rehab! Busted out? The ambulance left with Fletch inside.

"Three weeks." Archie huffed a sigh. "He definitely couldn't star as Nicholas, regardless." Archie shoved his hands into his pockets. "Well, that's the end of that, anyway. I guess I'll call Mayor Lang and tell her once and for all the play is off."

"No!" said Claire, Owen, and Portia all at the same time.

"No, Archie." Portia affected her most authoritative actress tone, the one she'd honed starring as Lena Lamont in *Singing in the Rain*. "You cast a male lead immediately or else."

"There isn't anyone." He looked wretched.

Portia pushed Owen forward. "Owen will do it. He's the obvious choice for Nicholas."

Owen? Portia was volunteering Owen to kiss Claire on stage?

Chapter 6

Owen

"If it will save the play." Owen pressed his fingertips into his temples. They stood on the doorstep of Portia's house, where she was looking up at him with admiring eyes. "I'll be happy to do it." If it would keep Portia around longer and help the town, Owen would throw himself to the wolves. "But you know I've got zero acting experience."

"I know what I saw when you were under the stage lights with Claire—the chemistry you created. Whoowee!" She fanned herself.

Owen gulped. "Chemistry?" Others had noticed?

"When I walked down the aisle of that theater, you could've cut it with a knife, my friend."

"Please." His face could've melted the snow. It hadn't been his intent to brew up anything onstage with Claire. Although, he couldn't deny that he and Claire had connected during the scene while playing the parts of Caroline and Nicholas—it was just awkward. "Anything you might have seen came from the script."

"I'm telling you, Owen. What you accomplished, that *bond* with the audience, was something most actors work years to achieve."

Whew. Owen exhaled. "With the audience. Of course."

"They were all holding their collective breath. I wish you could have felt it."

Well, he'd definitely felt something while holding Claire. When she'd called him Nicholas and claimed his love was the best gift she could imagine, that ridiculous paralysis had set in, with those harps' chords resonating through his whole being.

But that had been play-acting—literally! His subconscious mind should not mistake it for anything real.

"So, what I'm saying is I think you'll be a wonderful Nicholas." Portia stretched up on tiptoe and pressed a soft kiss to his cheek. "Don't worry, Claire will do fine as Caroline." She stepped back and spun in a circle, her skirts flying outward. "And I'm going to have wings!"

"Claire is making wings for your costume?"

As if she hadn't heard the question, Portia threw her arms around him. "You'll be the best Nicholas this town has ever seen. I'm telling everyone I know!"

Uh, no. Really, no. "No need to do that. My family—" His family was already side-eyeing him for not devoting enough of his time to Kingston Orchard, and for all the other things they hated him for right now. "Can we keep this under wraps?"

"Too late." Portia grinned. "I already posted lots of pics to my social media accounts. There are so many hearts! It's almost like when I posted that picture of me at the beach two years ago. Actually, I even got new followers after the picture of you and Claire got shared about fifty times."

"What picture of Claire and me?" His saliva turned to sand. "Portia, are you sure that was a good idea?" It might be bad. Very bad. For Claire. For him with his family. Even for Portia, if her boyfriend was seen having onstage chemistry with her best friend.

"Anything that gets chatter going about the play is good. There's no such thing as bad publicity, don't you know?"

That might be true in some circles, but Sugarplum Falls was not one of those circles. "What's done is done, I guess. But, hey. Before you post any more shots, double check with Archie, okay? And with me?"

"Oh, you're just being stodgy." She hugged him tightly. "But your stodginess makes you cuter." She said goodnight and went inside, leaving

Owen stodgy and cold on the doorstep.

Down at his work truck, he opened his phone and looked at Portia's social media account. Sure enough, there glowed a photo of Owen and Claire. The comments were all of a similar vein.

Hot!

C'est chouette!

He's slaying me with that smolder!

I'd give anything to swap places with Claire Downing right now. Why isn't she kissing him? I bet they totally made out the second they went off the stage. I bet fifty bucks they're making out right now.

I thought he was dating you, Portia. Are you really okay with this?

That had been Owen's question. He closed the feed. His phone rang at the same moment.

"Owen. Have you seen the photo?" Claire asked, her desperation palpable. "What are we going to do? Even if she takes it down, it's already been copied and shared fifty—nope, fifty-two times. It's hit half the world by now, but worse, *all* of Sugarplum Falls."

Huge exhale. "I just saw it." And he needed a cold shower. "It's something, all right."

"When did she even take the picture?" Claire sounded distraught. "I am really not crazy about the conversation it has sparked. On one of the posts they called me a—never mind."

"A what?" Someone was calling Claire names? That was going too far. None of this had been Claire's idea, and Owen's image was the one with the come-hither look in his eye. "Who called you something?"

"It's fine. It's fine. You and I and Portia know it's not true, so let's just forget about all that. I'm sorry I got you into this. I'm hanging up now."

"Hold up. You got me into this?" Hardly. "Wait—Claire!"

"What? There's nothing we can do but hope it blows over quickly." She sounded tired. There was a rhythmic humming, almost like a machine.

A sewing machine.

"Are you back at your shop? Working on costumes?"

"Do you *know* how many costumes there are for this play? Forty-one.

Plus the angel's costume."

With wings, apparently. "Can you delegate any?"

Claire sighed. "I probably could, if I had time. But if nobody ends up willing to help, I will have wasted precious time looking for another seamstress and explaining what needs to be done."

Whoa. "Maybe I could help."

"You're doing the sets. Please."

True. And ignoring the drama at the orchard. And in the library at the farmhouse, where Dad was lying inert, thanks to Owen.

"I did discover an upside."

"Oh, yeah?" Leave it to Claire to find an upside in the disaster. "What's that?"

"At least at night in the boutique I can rehearse my lines out loud while no customers can hear me stumbling over them."

The costumes *and* memorizing all the lines for the female lead. No question, Claire was bearing the majority burden of the work this play—probably investing more time than even Archie himself. "Maybe we should run lines together, since most of the scenes I'm in, so are you."

"Thanks. But don't you think being together at practices will be enough?"

There was a short timeline before the performances, and the lines had changed a lot from the original. "I'm not sure. A dual run-through wouldn't hurt, at least at first." Portia wouldn't mind. She could even join them.

"Well, Archie sent out a group text to the main characters to meet at his house tomorrow night to do our first read-through. Then we'll get an idea of how intense the memorization will be, right? But I've got this. I can insert it in my brain."

He pushed away his unexpected disappointment. "Well, if not, I'm here for you. Or, I should say, we're both here for Portia."

That earned him a laugh from Claire. "Yep. That's right."

They hung up.

Flipping her comment earlier, what had Owen gotten Claire into? She hadn't asked for this time-sucking vortex at Christmas, the biggest sales season for her boutique. Nor had she asked to be in the spotlight of the play, let alone a fifty-two-times-shared photo on social media.

The girl absolutely did not crave the spotlight. She was sacrificing too much, financially and emotionally, for the town's tradition's sake.

There's got to be a way to lighten her load.

Chapter 7

Claire

"All right, everyone." Archie clapped to get the cast's attention.

His kitchen's periphery was ringed with folding chairs, and the air smelled like mint and hot cocoa, which probably emanated from the tall cups labeled The Cider Press, Claire's favorite. A pile of cinnamon rolls from Sugarbabies Bakery graced the edge of Archie's countertop.

Ah, so he'd prepared as though he understood that these people needed to be bribed not to quit. Which probably wasn't wrong. Claire had been ready to quit before she auditioned.

"Find a chair and we'll get started on our get-to-know-you activities for the evening."

"Whatcha-ma-activities?" George Milliken, the nice Granddad from Angels Landing Bookstore, asked. "I thought this was a read-through of the script."

"It is, it is. Well, it was going to be." Archie found a seat, and Portia parked herself beside him. He wore his signature cardigan sweater, and for whatever reason, Portia had dressed to match him tonight. "In the theater, cast unity is very important. If we want to perfect our chemistry on stage, we need to create some off stage."

Echoes of Fletch's speech from the alleyway rang in the air. Claire stuck a finger in her ear as if to stop the awful clanging. Archie couldn't possibly be doing this based on advice from Fletch Fletcher!

"Now, many of you have heard the last-minute change in casting. Due to unforeseen circumstances, Owen Kingston will now be our Nicholas."

A few cast members clapped.

"First, we'll go around the circle and everyone will give their name and their theater experience."

Oh, brother. That took a full twenty minutes, even though there were only two dozen people in the kitchen, which opened up into the living room. Claire and Owen both admitted this was their first play, which earned them blank stares, and one set of dagger-looks from the sparkly Donny and Marie Gatwick. One guy, cast as mayor in the play, had a nice singing voice and had performed as an understudy in an off-Broadway production of *Holiday Inn,* in which his late wife had been the lead. Then, the Gatwicks detailed their decade of stage experience in high school drama and past town Christmas plays.

Owen leaned in and whispered, "How on earth did Archie choose us over them?"

Beside Claire, George Milliken answered, and not in the quietest voice. "It's because of that sizzling moment the two of you had on the stage."

Wrong, since Archie had cast Fletch, initially. At least there was that consolation.

But if everyone thought Claire was working up chemistry with her friend, who was also her best friend's boyfriend, yikes. Please, let her get out of here fast.

"Next, we're going to dig deep." Archie beamed, as if he'd just promised everyone real gold coins in their Christmas stockings, not the chocolate kind wrapped in stamped gold foil. "Pair up. You and your partner will bond."

Bond. *Bond?* Oh, dear. Claire didn't have time for this. Nor did she long to bond. She wanted to memorize lines and get back to the sewing machine.

Owen gripped Claire's elbow. "I'm pairing with you."

"But ... what about Portia? Owen—"

However, Claire's protest died when Archie said, "As director, I'll pair

51

with our narrator."

Claire couldn't suppress her grimace. Archie, making his move. And in front of everyone! It was brazen. Portia shouldn't put up with it.

"Then we'll have Caroline and Nicholas paired." He sent them a pointed look, as if commanding them to bond.

But they were already friends. Close friends. Didn't she know everything she needed to about Owen as it was? "Maybe we should bond somewhere else. Like, me at my shop with the fabric, and you working on the set pieces."

But Archie wouldn't have that. He named the other cast members and their assigned counterparts. "First, you'll talk about three simple, easy facts about yourself. Anything that your partner might not know about you yet. Then, as promised, I'm asking you to *dig deep*. Discuss with your partner the thing that is bothering you most right now."

As in, Archie's get-to-know-you exercise and the fact we aren't getting on with rehearsals for the play? The frown on her face was probably a buzz-kill, so she wiped it off and affected a pleasant expression. With effort.

Of course, since she'd be with Owen, it couldn't be that bad. In fact, it might be pretty good. *Except, what if he tells me that his biggest bother is the fact I looked at him with wanton eyes the other day? Or that he's read the comments now and agrees, I'm a witch.* "Now, don't confine yourselves to these uncomfortable folding chairs. Find anywhere you like to converse." Archie took Portia by the elbow, and in a lower but still audible voice said, "Come with me." He led her out of the kitchen and down the hallway to the bedroom side of the house.

If Owen noticed, he wasn't showing any signs of irritation.

Maybe he really did deserve the role of Nicholas for those acting skills. That, or, more likely, he didn't consider Archie Holdaway any kind of threat. He was Owen Kingston, after all.

"Porch swing?" Owen asked. "It's cold outside, but it's loud in here and out there at least we could hear each other talk." From the countertop, he pulled two tall cups of cocoa from The Cider Press, handing Claire one. He led the way out to Archie's generous front porch with wide, white-painted wood planks and a matching swing. The cushions on the swing were red and green, and Christmas lights wrapped every rail and pillar of the fence around the porch.

"Is it just me, or ..." Claire sat beside him, and the chains squeaked as Owen gently rocked them forward and back.

"Or, what?"

"Shouldn't we be reading through the script?" Claire sipped her cocoa. Mmm. Hers had a mint add-in. Delicious. "There isn't actually a lot of time for dilly-dallying."

"Eyes on the prize, Claire." Owen sipped his cocoa. "Meaning, this is going to both save the play's tradition and keep Portia in town. In fact, she looked really happy tonight."

Weirdly true, but Portia had always derived energy from being in a role. "Let's get started. Three things and then a concern? That's the format?"

"It's hard, since I feel like we already know each other pretty well." Owen shrugged and sipped. "How's this going to work?"

They did know each other pretty well. After years together, they'd told each other most of the anecdotes of their lives. "Maybe if we make it Christmas-specific, we can come up with something new. Keep it festive."

"Festive, huh?" Owen's boot slipped from the porch, and the swing bumped. He bobbled his hot cocoa, but he lunged to keep it upright. It left him sitting a little closer to Claire. She didn't move. He didn't move. Then, Claire *couldn't* move. She couldn't breathe, in fact.

He's not sliding away. His leg is touching mine. She swallowed hard. "Okay, I'm first." She talked as fast as if she were auditioning for a job as an auctioneer. "At Christmas, my favorite treat isn't the usual sugar cookies or pecan pie that everyone else seems to love. I have a secret craving for those cardamom doughnuts that Mrs. Toledo makes at Sugarbabies Bakery, and on my way to the shop every morning, I stop in and get one. Sometimes I get two. Then, I eat them slowly throughout the whole day. I don't know who else in the world likes cardamom and nutmeg, but I'm addicted, and she only makes them at Christmas, and I can't seem to get enough of them. Some days, it's the only thing I eat, if I'm really busy. But they're delicious and they should be elevated to standard holiday food status in every home worldwide."

53

A smile tugged at the side of Owen's mouth. In a slow, lazy drawl he said, "Sounds delicious. I've never tried them, but I like the ones my mom makes."

"Your mom?"

"She makes spice cake doughnuts at Christmas, too. Sometimes she adds cloves. I'll bring you some."

"I—I'd like that. Cloves would taste good. Ha, my mom can't bake her way out of a paper bag. But you don't have to do that for me."

"I want to. And my mom would be happy to teach you to make them, if you want."

Oh, no. Claire couldn't hog all Mrs. Kingston's time. She had enough to do with her own large family's needs. But, "That is a sweet thought."

"It's more than a thought. Kingstons are doers, not just thinkers." His face clouded. "Most of the time."

True. His whole extended family had been struggling since Granddad Kingston's death last Christmas, and Owen's dad's illness. Owen didn't talk much about it, but Claire caught snippets now and then. In fact, Owen had taken Claire and Portia to the hospital to visit him on Sunday afternoons before the family had brought him home to convalesce.

Seeing someone as big and strong as John Kingston hooked up to machines for tasks as simple as breathing and eating was really tough. Likely much tougher for Owen. In fact, he seemed more distressed over it than he really should. The coma wasn't Owen's fault.

"What are your other two Christmas factoids? I liked the first one." Owen took another swig of cocoa. "Take your time, though. I'm still thinking about what I can say."

"I'm struggling here, too."

"How about *most embarrassing Christmas memory*?"

"Easy." Claire cringed as the memory jarred loose. "I was the seamstress for my elementary school class's Christmas play in sixth grade."

"You were already sewing then?"

"Wait until you hear the story." The tale still made her face burn. "One of the costumes, for the guy who dressed as the chief elf, I couldn't finish in time.

My mom suggested I get the glue gun and put the trim on his tunic that way. But during the play, it caught on the Christmas tree and unraveled, leaving a long trail of white behind him. The kids figured out how to turn that into some kind of elf-related potty joke, and I swore I'd never make another costume."

And yet, here she was: drowning in theater costumes again.

"What made you break your promise?"

"My mom didn't let me wallow. She set me up with even more sewing lessons. I babysat for a lady in exchange for her teaching me lots of different stitches. Then, once I improved beyond the basics, I was hooked."

Owen nodded. "You were confident."

Huh. Maybe so. She'd never really considered herself one of those Confident People, the kind who drew people in with charisma, but when it came to sewing—yeah. She knew her way around needle and thread.

"Those dresses you designed. You really ought to put them out in the store."

Um, no. Not yet. Maybe not ever. "Here's my last factoid." Her final tale was kind of a cop-out. "My Christmas dream is to have a daughter someday and wear a matching dress with her to church on a Sunday in December."

Owen should have been chuckling at the shallowness of Claire's dream. But instead, he was nodding. "My mom did that with my older sister Odessa when she was young."

"Yeah, it's weird because my mom got matching Christmas dresses with my older sister, and then much later with my younger sister, but—"

"But?"

"But, when I would have been the right age to match dresses with her, that's when Dad left. There were no funds for matching dresses, and Mom lost a lot of weight after the divorce. She didn't fit in the dress she'd worn with Taylor, and then, by the time Bailee was old enough, she was in a better place emotionally and financially, so she did the dress thing again."

"That must have made you feel left out."

Totally. Utterly. But she laughed it off. "Plight of the middle child." She steeled her smile into place. "And why I am going to do it with my daughters. *All* of them."

55

"All, huh? How many kids do you want?"

Claire froze again. "Um …"

"Kinda personal?" Owen ventured. "I thought we were *digging deep* here." He chuckled. "But I understand if it's too personal. We're not actually a couple."

All his words jumbled in her mind. The implications of them tangled up. The press of his thigh against hers, through his jeans and her trousers, created a little burning sensation along the side of her leg, while his words burned little holes in her thoughts.

"Either four or six," she blurted.

"Kids?" Owen set his cup to the side. "That's a lot for these days."

"Two isn't enough, though."

"Two does seem scant." He nodded. "Not enough noise around the house. And what if they don't get along? There's no backup sibling."

Right? "Eight might be too many, even for me."

"I'm getting an *even number* vibe here."

"Exactly."

"You don't want anyone to have to be the middle child." Owen put an arm around her shoulders. Its weight and heat seeped into her. "That's thoughtful." He tugged her a little closer, and thunder rumbled in her chest. "You're already thinking about your future children's needs. I like that."

Claire liked something—a lot. It was probably Owen's cologne. At least her hormones did. At this proximity, it mixed with his own scent and the night air to create some kind of heady mixture of manly pheromones she should *not* be aware of. "It's your turn," she squeaked out, begging the air to be full of something besides just Owen's allure. Words might help.

"Me? But you didn't say what's bothering you most right now." Owen didn't pull away, and there was no way on earth Claire could answer *you're bothering me most. You and your sexy scent and your kind words and your complete unavailability. It's bothering me to high heaven.*

Claire shook her head. "Oh, we already discussed that—my mom's challenge to try something new so I can make some permanent friendships."

"Don't you think of Portia and me as *permanent?*"

56

To be honest, Claire couldn't think of much that was coherent other than how wrong she was at her very core for being affected by Owen's combo of kindness and Axe Body Wash, or whatever it was. "Sure, but also no. You have each other."

Owen pulled his arm off Claire's shoulder and slid back a little. *Whew.*

"Right. Yeah." He kind of shook himself. "And you need backups. Like an additional sibling."

"Or three. Yeah. So, what about you?" Owen had better deliver. Claire had more or less bared her soul to him with the lonely middle child thing—which hadn't been her intention. But somehow it felt okay to tell Owen those little parts of her that she'd bottled up and hidden for a long time. Like a burden discussed was a burden lifted. Shared. "And if you're even considering holding back, forget it. Remember, we're *digging deep*."

"Oh, I've got my shovel here. Believe me, Claire Downing."

Chapter 8

Owen

The porch swing creaked, and the temperature had to be in the single digits as the snow fell in faint flurries, but he wasn't cold. For whatever reason, being outside with Claire didn't chill him like it should have.

It was the hot cocoa. Not having Claire nearby. Totally.

"Are you sure you're ready for this?" he asked. After what Claire had shared with him, such heartfelt stories from her past—a couple of them veering that way unintentionally it had seemed—he couldn't just phone it in for this activity by naming his favorite Christmas candy and what he'd wanted as a gift when he was ten years old.

"Your turn. And if you're even considering holding back, forget it. Remember, we're *digging deep*."

"I'm ready to dig." He made a shoveling pantomime. Cheesy. But Claire didn't ever seem to mind cheese. "Let's get very deep here." He slid close to her once again. A moment ago, he'd pulled away from her. There'd been a movement at the curtain, and if Portia had looked out the window to see Owen with his arm around Claire, she might not have reacted as nonchalantly as she should've. Owen and Claire were friends. He'd been comforting her, nothing more.

But she does smell like vanilla candles. Owen was a lifelong fan of vanilla candles. A chance to smell them should not be passed up.

"Have I told you that this Christmas I'm expecting to become an uncle? Odessa and Heath are having a baby girl."

"Common knowledge is not the same as *digging deep*. Count me unimpressed."

"Are you saying a baby isn't impressive?"

"A baby is the most impressive thing in the universe, but it's not *digging deep* if you tell me that as your Christmas secret." Claire laughed. "Although, I personally can't wait to see that little one. Are they going to name her after you? Owenasa?"

That was a good one. "Owenina."

"Really?" Claire's eyes grew wide. "Are you being serious?"

"Of course not. My sister Odessa is so busy being in love with Heath Sutherland and caught up in her wife life and impending mommy-hood to remember I exist. She barely calls me more than once a week these days."

"See?" Claire murmured.

"See what?"

"People who get married don't end up being a permanent part of your daily life anymore."

Warm realization rushed through him. "I get it now." No wonder Claire wanted more people. If Owen was going to keep moving in the direction of marrying Portia, Claire's concerns made total sense. "Look, if there's anything I think of to help you with your concern, I'm going to do it. I promise."

"Thanks, Owen, but it's really something I should do for myself."

Unless he could think of some good guy to set her up with—then he could help. But who? Who would be good enough for Claire?

"Can we get back to talking about you again, pal? This weather is the kind of temperature where people's toes turn black and fall off."

"Are you cold?"

Claire met his gaze. Her pale green eyes were conflicted. "Truthfully? No."

Owen, in fact, was a little warmer than he had been a minute ago. "Okay, okay. Here are my three things." He told her quickly about the Christmas as a kid when he'd received a scooter, but the snow was too deep and the wheels iced up, and then he lost it in the snow and couldn't find it until the spring thaw. "I was so worried that Mom and Dad would get mad, that I didn't tell them about it until about three years ago."

She whisper-laughed. "What did they say when you told them?"

"They're Kingstons. They laughed themselves sick." As Kingstons tended to do. "It wasn't even that funny."

"It's really not," but Claire was laughing a little, with her glove in front of her mouth. "I don't know why I'm laughing."

"Some people." He poked her ribs with his free hand, but it moved him closer to her again. "Fine. Can we agree you guys are all mean-spirited for making fun of a scared kid who lost his present from Santa in the snow?"

"Total agreement." She was still giggling. "I'm sorry. I don't know why I'm laughing." It was shaking the porch swing. "I'll get ahold of myself, I swear. As soon as I stop picturing you in your little kid snowsuit trying to ride a scooter and riding it straight into a snowdrift."

Hey. Not nice. But kind of a funny image. "Whatever. No wonder you and my mom get along famously." They both loved sewing and Sugarplum Falls, for one. And making fun of Owen, for another. "Should I go on, or is one laugh-a-thon enough for one night?"

"Please." Claire's laughter subsided at last. "Continue." She offered him the royal hand-wave roll. "I'm all ears."

"You mentioned your favorite Christmas food, so I'll tell you mine is berry pie with tons of whipped cream."

"We had that at my house during the Supper Club of Doom."

"You make a mean berry pie."

"The way you said it, it sounds like mean-berry is a kind of berry." She looked up at him and grinned, the pink gloss of her lips catching the porch light. Owen licked his lips involuntarily. Claire, to his heart-rate's detriment, mirrored it. Her voice lowered. "All those mean berries."

Owen pulled back and cleared his throat, tugging at his collar where suddenly his scarf was too constricting. "Right."

Claire did have full, tempting lips. They were like sugarplums. *And I'm going to have to kiss them while practicing for this play—more than once. More than twice.* He felt his Adam's apple rise and fall.

"Got a resolution about how you'll do Christmas in the future?" she asked from somewhere really far away. "Like my matching dresses thing?"

He snapped back from the land of make-out-on-stage fantasies. "I, yeah. Uh, sure. I want to take my kids sledding on Christmas. Or at least during Christmas break every year. There's a hill on the far side of the orchard that Granddad refused to plant out with trees. He had it cleared just for sledding. We grew up with toboggans and big tire inner-tubes and sledded and then ate chili and doughnuts with all the cousins and aunts and uncles. Big family fun. We still do it every year."

"Were they spice doughnuts?"

"Mostly just glazed doughnuts from the grocery store. But if you wanted spiced, I bet my mom would make some special for you that day. It'll be really fun. You'll love it."

"Um, what?" Claire was looking at him like he'd just spoken Swahili.

He reviewed his last statement. *It sounded like I was asking her on the family sledding trip.* But why not? "I mean it. You'll love it."

"Owen, I—"

Then it dawned on him. No one in the Kingston family had mentioned the sledding day yet. It hadn't happened last year. The funeral had overshadowed the sledding day.

Maybe it wouldn't happen. Maybe none of the Kingstons' extended family traditions would continue, now that Granddad was gone. *And Dad is out of commission.* So much tension, so little connectedness.

"You're right. I shouldn't have promised you a day of big family fun when I'm not able to guarantee it will actually happen. Which brings me to the biggest thing bothering me these days." He set his empty cocoa cup on the ground and rubbed his head. "I'm not sure any of the Kingston family events are a go for this year, actually."

Claire rested her hand atop his on his knee. "You've got a big weight on your shoulders—running the orchard *and* being the de facto head of the family. A family as big as yours, it's got to be quite the burden."

61

Indeed. And it was worse, thanks to the situation he'd caused that had placed him there. He grimaced. "If only there were a way to unite us somehow. It's been a year. A hard year. Nothing's the same."

There he went, spewing out all his feelings. None of this had been his plan. He'd planned to say, *My biggest bother is that Archie Holdaway dude, who's hitting on my woman all the time,* and then laugh it off when Claire reassured him that Archie didn't compare to him. Because, Claire would have said that, right? Promised him that Portia wasn't interested in Archie but only had eyes for Owen?

Instead, there he was, blabbing on about Kingston family politics. Exposing their dirty laundry to someone outside the family circle. Was it disloyal of him to do so? Possibly. Probably. But somehow, he'd needed to air his grievance, and Claire was such a great listener.

"I did have one idea, but—"

"Yeah?" Owen lifted his head and turned to her. "I'm listening." That's right, they'd been washing dishes at her house when he'd mentioned it earlier, and she'd had an idea, but they'd been interrupted. "What is it? And remember, you're not butting in. You're supporting me. There's a big difference."

"If you're sure."

He was.

"You know how you have the trees decorated with Christmas lights all around the playground at the orchard?"

"Sure."

"Who puts those lights up every year?"

"Generally, I hire out. We have a lot of seasonal workers in the orchard, but after harvest some of them stay in Sugarplum Falls, so I try to offer them work hours if I have some. They hang lights."

"What if you expanded the light show? What if you got your in-town seasonal workers to help some, but you enlisted the help of all the Kingstons?"

"Expanded the lights?"

"I mean …" Claire bit her lower lip, like she often did while she was thinking. "How about filling as much of the orchard as possible with lights?"

"There are about a thousand acres of trees." Did she have any idea how many trees that would be? It was enough to keep the West Coast and Intermountain West in apples and stone fruits. "Seems like …"

"Not all the trees. Just enough that it becomes something the family can work on together. You know, maybe as a way to honor your Granddad's memory."

Owen chewed on the idea for a few moments before answering. "The Orchard Walk that's always been set up around the playground area was his idea to start with." He chewed some more, and the more he thought about it, the more it blossomed in his mind. Like the flowers on the apricot trees in the spring.

"If you don't want to, it's just an idea."

"No, actually. It's good. Claire, you're good." Really good. He put his arm around her again and pulled her close. Then, in a fit of impulse, he pressed a kiss to her soft, vanilla-scented cheek. "Thanks."

"Well, well." Portia sauntered up, patting her mittens together. "If there's one thing I can say for Archie Holdaway, it's that he definitely knows how to inspire his actors to bond."

63

Chapter 9

Claire

Tremors from last night's horror show kept Claire's fingers clumsy all morning at Apple Blossom Boutique as she ruined more than one yard of white felt meant to become spats, but which would languish in the Sugarplum Falls junkyard forever more, after being subjected to Claire's spasms of guilt.

I shouldn't have been sitting that close to him. I shouldn't have let him keep his arm around me like that. Even though it had only been a few seconds between the half-hug and The Kiss That Portia Saw, and there'd been no way to see it coming, Claire still wanted the floor to swallow her whole every time she thought of it.

Which—yeah. It had been all day. Every minute.

Oh, but Owen had smelled heavenly. If she'd tried to even think about preventing that quick graze of his lips to her cheek and then her temple, she probably couldn't have. Her head had been too swirly with his cologne.

Again—not cool. Friendship with him or not, romantically he belonged to Portia. And Portia was Claire's best friend. They were all friends.

Then again, Owen had *intended* that moment as a gesture of friendship—only Claire had been confused, no one else.

Portia had immediately discerned the situation, and she'd pulled Owen to his feet, thrown her arms around his neck and told him she was so grateful for

64

all he was doing to save the play.

Then, she'd hugged Claire, too. Terrible, horrible, no-good, very bad Claire. Who had let her mind get distracted, if only briefly. It wasn't like she was *interested* in Owen. They were buddies. Owen knew that. Claire knew that. Portia knew that. It had been Claire's hormones that were confused, and only for a second.

Thank goodness.

That said, the bonding had definitely worked. Their friendship and connection had grown from strands to thin cables, for sure.

But, now that they'd bonded, and her hormones had attempted one massive defection from her brain's command ... what about kissing him on stage?

Her sewing machine's foot pedal sank too quickly, and she sent the seam askew.

Dang it.

The Apple Blossom Boutique's front doors jingled, signaling a customer's entry. Claire should go greet whoever it was, and give her eyes a break from the stitches.

"Cliff, how are you?"

Cliff Rockingham, owner of the best hotel Sugarplum Falls, Sweetwater Hotel, pressed a finger to the center of his forehead.

"Not good, I take it?"

"I drew my sister Lark's name for Christmas gift exchange."

Lark—yeah. Claire knew all about how picky Cliff's sister was. "I just got some new angora scarves with matching berets in. Do you think she'd like that?"

"Angora?" Cliff's icy-blue eyes lit up, and the wrinkle between his brows relaxed. "I should have asked you first, before I worried for three weeks about this."

If only Cliff had auditioned for the Christmas play—and not Fletcher the Lecher. *Or Owen—then I wouldn't be in the hot water I'm in.* "I saw some work trucks at Sweetwater Hotel when I passed by on my way into town. Are you catching the remodeling bug, too?"

65

He sighed heavily. "It's going around, isn't it? But no. Sweetwater Hotel has its clientele."

"Right. It doesn't need to compete with cozy bed and breakfasts like Gingerbread Inn. You're set."

"Uh-huh." He didn't sound set. He sounded concerned.

Cliff bought the scarf for his sister and then left with a "Merry Christmas" to Claire and Lulu that didn't sound quite merry enough—at least not for Lulu's taste, apparently.

Lulu shook her head, clicking her teeth. "That man works too hard."

"He needs a big plate of cookies from Sugarbabies Bakery." Cookies healed so many things.

"He *needs* a date." Lulu wagged a finger at him, as if he'd done something wrong by still being a single man at his advanced age of—what? Thirty?

"Lulu, you know Cliff's history."

"Everyone knows it—but getting left at the altar by that interloping, gold-digging redhead *years ago* isn't a good excuse for staying single in Sugarplum Falls. Mayor Lang is going to train her sights on Cliff Rockingham before you know it. He'd better watch his back for a big, fat target."

"Lulu!" Claire let out a gasp. "Let's not wish that on anyone!" *Including me.* "Some wounds take a long time to heal." Especially broken hearts after a childhood like Cliff's. Losing both parents at once? He'd been such a mensch for taking such good care of his younger siblings, when Cliff had been nothing more than a kid himself. "We're not putting a timeline on his return to the land of relationships. Not you, not me, not even Lisa Lang."

Claire went back to her sewing machine, but a few seconds later, Lulu appeared at the workroom door. "Claire? Were you expecting your mom today?"

Mom! Claire clutched at her heart. "Is she here?" She shot from her seat and hustled to the shop floor, where she threw her arms around Mom's neck. "It's been forever!"

"Yeah, a couple of months." Mom hugged back for a moment. "Time flies."

66

No, it didn't. Not when Claire was alone with no family around. "I wasn't expecting you today." Or any of the times Mom returned to Sugarplum Falls. She loved a drop-in visit most of all. She thought of surprises as the best gifts, so she never called ahead.

"Well, you came to our house for Thanksgiving, so I figured it was my turn to take the mountain pass trek. I hear avalanches are possible, though, so I'm only staying until this evening. Besides, I needed to shop for a dress for Eddy's work dinner, and yours is my favorite shop."

Eddy. That's what she called Neville Edwards, her husband. It'd be a while before Claire could call him a stepdad. For now, he was Mom's husband. Why did Claire find it so hard to connect with everyone?

Stupid shyness.

"Do you have anything in black or red or green?"

Claire did, and she took Mom to look over all the semi-formal racks of gowns. "How's this one? It comes in Christmas colors."

"I'm looking for something truly unique. Something no one else has." She nudged Claire's ribcage. "You know what I am getting at."

Claire did know. "Mom, they're just not ready." *I'm just not ready.* "How's this eggplant one? It'll bring out the green of your eyes."

"Sweetheart ..." Mom let the word hang, and then she tried on the fit-and-flare dress with the puffed sleeves. "It's great. Not as great as a Claire Original, of course, but I'll take it."

"I'll put the dresses in the shop when I'm ready." Which was probably never.

"Honey"—Mom lowered her voice—"you have real talent. A light. Don't hide it under a bushel, or on a storeroom shelf. A woman feels so good about herself in an amazing dress. You can give lots of women that gift."

Not yet, she couldn't. Maybe someday. When an alien inhabited her body. A confident one. "Thanks, Mom. I'll think about it."

"Don't wait too long." Mom handed Claire the dress to box up. "By the way, sorry the dinner didn't pan out like you'd hoped."

Understatement of the season. "I'm still trying something new, though. I promise I'm not letting you down."

"Oh, I know that." Mom's eye twinkled.

Tissue paper crinkled in Claire's grip. "You know about the play?"

"I never pictured you as an aspiring actress, but once I saw that photograph on Portia's social media, the one with you and that Kingston fellow, I started thinking maybe you'd missed your big calling in life."

She'd seen the photo! All the way in Darlington. If only there were a way to burn down all social media. "It was an audition. Portia shouldn't have taken that photograph, let alone posted it. You do know Owen is Portia's boyfriend these days, don't you?"

"Of course, of course." Mom accepted the Apple Blossom Boutique box from Claire's hands. "But that doesn't mean the two of you can't look well-cast as love interests during a play. All the comments under the share of the photo I saw gave you high praise as an actress. One guy even said he wished he could find you and ask you out, asked if anyone had your number. Isn't that sweet?"

"Sweet!"

"I love you darling. You're better at a lot more things than you think." Mom came around and gave her a hug. "Give yourself a chance to be happy. That's the real new thing I'm hoping you'll try."

Why were tears stinging her eyes? At work, no less. "It's nice to have someone on my side."

Because the truth was, everyone else who'd come into Apple Blossom Boutique lately *hadn't* been on Claire's side. Instead, they'd shot Claire surreptitious glances and whispered to each other about whether Claire was *A*, pursuing her own best friend's boyfriend, *B*, the luckiest girl in the world to have the heir of Kingston Orchards look at her like that, or *C*, pretty enough to think she could steal someone else's man.

Exhausting. One photo, in her case, was apparently worth ten million gossipy words.

Mom stood at the exit. "Can you come to dinner with me when you get off work?"

"If we make it fast. Archie Holdaway needs us for a read-through at the Kingston Theater." Finally, the actual read-through. They should've done it last night, instead of putting Claire into dangerously close proximity with Owen's pheromones.

"Archie! Didn't he have the most incapacitating crush on Portia for years? They dated, and he dumped her when she moved to the coast."

"That's the guy."

"Isn't Owen worried about that?"

"Owen? Why would he be? He's Owen Kingston." The closest living thing to the Nicholas character he was assigned to portray in the town Christmas play. "Owen never needs to worry about any man stealing his girl."

Mom shrugged. "I'll see you at six, then. Bring anyone you like. I'd love to see Owen and Portia. I miss his mom and aunts. And lots of people in Sugarplum Falls."

"I hope you miss me the most."

"Of course, dear." Mom blew a kiss and left.

Long days. Such long days. Plus, the nights with her backside glued to the sewing chair. Exhausting was the only word for it.

Claire raced back to her tasks. Every second away from them she was burning daylight. Not that daylight was her only sewing time. She'd more or less worked all night the past few nights on the costumes here in the boutique.

There was no other choice.

"Hey?" Lulu peeked into the workroom again a few minutes later, looking nervous. "You weren't home last night when I stopped by to drop off banana bread. At least you didn't come to the door."

"What time did you come?" Like that would have mattered. "Thanks for the thought, though." She loved banana bread.

"Late. Like, almost ten, but I know you're a night owl."

"Nah, I was still here sewing until the wee hours." And yes, she had ended up sleeping in her office on the sofa and only popping home for a half-hour this morning to shower and change. It was ridiculous. "I did finish three children's vests, including sewing on all the buttons, and a few pairs of the spats to cover the men's shoes."

"It's a shame about the flood in the theater ruining everything from props to costumes to the curtains to the carpets. It's funny, though. I could've sworn I

69

heard someone at your house. I thought it was strange that you didn't come to the door."

"Even if I'd had to come to the door in a robe, I would have answered it for you, Lulu. You're Lulu."

"I know, right? You did come to the door that one time I stopped by when you were in the bathtub, which is why this time I waited so long after I heard the ruckus inside."

"Ruckus?" Claire went cold from head to toe. "What kind of ruckus?"

"Oh, like pots and pans clanging. Some muffled hollering from the ceiling—or the roof. Not sure. Maybe a little bit of kicking at concrete. That type of noise."

"Lulu! What on earth?"

"I mean, I did call the police."

"The police!"

"Yeah, they came and heard it, too, but when they looked in the house, and you weren't there, the sounds quieted, and they didn't find anything. Super strange."

Claire gripped the countertop near the cash register. "Lulu. What time is it now?"

"Four in the afternoon."

"You didn't think to tell me this before now?"

"You ... were sewing. Very intensely. And I didn't want to worry you."

"Worry me! You're totally freaking me out. There's no *worry* here. It's utter panic." Her breath came quickly, and she had to tell herself to control it. Ten thousand questions blossomed. "Why didn't I hear anything about it from the police? Why didn't they keep looking for ... whatever made the sound? Did they draw any conclusions? Like, did an animal get in my house?"

No damage or noise had caught her attention as Claire had rushed through the house to change and shower during the wee hours. But good grief!

"I mean, because the noise stopped when they arrived, and I didn't really have any proof, they gave me one of those, *you're crazy, lady* looks and said they'd file a report and contact you later. How was I supposed to assume the evidence would disappear?" Lulu's face burned. "To tell you the truth, I was

70

too embarrassed to tell you about it, which is the reason I delayed mentioning it. Maybe you don't believe me either. The police asked to take my blood-alcohol levels. My husband told me I was a Gladys Kravitz, that nosy neighbor character from *Bewitched* on TV, going around peeking in other people's windows at night. He also said I shouldn't bake after eight p.m. anymore." She hiccupped.

Claire stood and gathered Lulu in her arms. "You were just trying to do the right thing."

"I can tell from the tone of your voice you don't believe me either." Lulu's voice quavered. "But I'm not making it up. It was windy last night, but that wasn't the night wind."

Last night had definitely been windy, though. "I do have a couple of tin pans in my chimney that blow in the wind to discourage bats from taking up residence. Could that be what you heard?"

"Now you sound like the police."

"I'm sorry. I do believe you heard something. I'll go check it out." Right now, so she could concentrate on the costumes again without worrying. Lack of concentration messed up stitches. Claire grabbed her parka from the coat tree.

"Don't do it alone!" Lulu gasped and clutched her throat. "He might be strong. Or dangerous."

"Who?"

"The man I heard in your house."

The front door had jingled a moment ago, and Owen Kingston walked in. He wore a jacket that hugged his narrow hips and stretched across his shoulders. How Archie could have ever assigned the role of Nicholas to Fletcher the Lecher over Owen in the first place was a complete mystery— Owen possessed the exact body-type of a classic idealized male. Strong. Broad where he should be broad and narrow where he should be narrow.

Objectively speaking.

He shoved something into his pocket.

"There was a man in your house?" Owen asked, striding toward Claire and Lulu. "Who? Not that I should be surprised." He turned to Lulu. "Men

71

should be lined up at Claire's door begging to date her." He reverted to Claire again. "But who did you let inside? What guy could meet your standards?"

What was that supposed to mean? Claire's mouth went dry. Owen both thought Claire's standards were too high—and that guys should want to date her?

Hardy-har-har. To both. She was a shy girl who rarely got asked out, even by guys who'd test the limits of her standards levels.

Lulu jumped in. "I was just telling Claire about the crazy thing that happened last night when I stopped by her place pretty late." Lulu recounted her story, leaving out the parts where the police officers had asked for blood tests and her husband had doubted her. "It was definitely weird. Worse, she thinks she's going to go check it out alone."

Owen straightened up tall and his gaze snapped over to Claire. "No."

"No, what?" Claire shook her head. "I'm just going to see if I can hear the sounds."

"Fine, but I'm coming with." Owen took her by the arm and marched her toward the exit. He had a firm grip, one that penetrated through her sweater and warmed her.

"Don't worry," Lulu called. "I'll hold down the fort while you two go vindicate me. And you'd better vindicate me!" The door to the shop shut as Lulu made her final request, muffling her voice.

Out in the street, Owen let go of Claire's arm. She rolled her shoulder to shrug off Owen's warm touch—which, yeah. They should really institute a hands-off policy.

Especially since that rogue little part of Claire didn't mind it. Not one bit.

Owen would never look at me. He only has eyes for Portia.

Just like guys always only ever had eyes for Portia when they met Claire and her best friend. Claire was more than used to it by now. The dark-haired beauty, with her mystery and flirtation skills, drew them like moths to a porch light. Men never even saw Claire when Portia was in the room. Portia always included Claire, of course, brought her to everything fun, made sure she had a date of her own. But even Claire's assigned dates were always enthralled with Portia's charisma.

72

Whether or not Owen had said guys should be lining up to date Claire.

"You don't have to come with me as I go in search of Lulu's vindication. I'm sure you have better places to be."

"If there's an intruder in your house and I let you go in there alone, and say he's dangerous, what kind of a friend would I be?"

"Fine. Have it your way." Claire double-wrapped her scarf.

"No sense taking two cars. Ride with me." Owen held the passenger side door of his truck open for her, and Claire climbed in. She'd ridden in this work truck dozens of times, but always in the crew row of the cab lately, while Portia occupied the passenger seat beside Owen. Owen paused, holding his phone after starting the engine. "I'll just text Portia and tell her to meet us over there instead of at your shop."

"What brought you by my store anyway?" It couldn't have been instinct that she was in distress. "You were carrying something earlier."

"Oh, right. That was from Archie. Measurements for Portia's costume." He cleared his throat and flexed his fingers on the wheel. "She said she needed updated measurements, and that they needed to be accurate."

"So, Archie took them?" Why wouldn't Archie just text them over to Claire? "I'm missing something."

"Yeah, I think after the debacle with the audition photos being splashed all over social media, Archie isn't allowing anything digital to be connected with the play. No photos of anything at all."

Oh, brother. "So you ended up as courier?"

"I was across the street from the high school anyway to drop off my nephew's lunch sack at the elementary school. My sister said he forgot it this morning, and I was heading into town, and—"

Didn't he have a vast operation with thousands of acres and scores of employees to manage as his day job? But Owen was a nice guy and wanted to help his sister, as well as make sure his nephew had lunch. "Which nephew?"

"Ellis."

"Ohhh, Ellis." Claire probably wore a goofy grin.

"So you know why I can't just let him miss a meal on my watch." He got a goofy grin of his own.

73

"Your sister's got the cutest kids on the planet."

"Yeah, I'm pretty lucky to live close to them and have them in my life."

Just when Owen Kingston couldn't be any more like the character Nicholas in the town play, he went all goo-goo eyed over his nieces and nephews. Heaven help women everywhere dying of envy that his heart was already taken by Portia Sutherland.

Of course, heaven *shouldn't* help the women who accused Claire of trying to steal him. They were just jealous jerks.

"Oh, and there's another reason I came in, but I can do it later." They motored down Orchard Street toward the Downing house. "I promised my sister I'd ask you a favor—can she have first pick at the newest shipment of mother-daughter dresses this season?"

"I'm happy to let her come in before shop hours to look." Wow. Claire was a topic of conversation in the Kingston family?

"It's nice to have at least one family member besides my parents not grousing at me day and night," he said darkly. "But enough about that." He brightened and handed her a sheet of paper. "Here are those measurements from Archie and Portia."

She looked them over. "Wow. Comprehensive." Especially for a flowing robe costume that would only really require a few strategic measurements, like Portia's height and the length of her spine to her waist. Hmm, there were six or seven crossed out bust measurements before a final one was circled.

Fishy?

They pulled up at Claire's little brick house. Nothing looked amiss in the daylight.

Also, Mom's car wasn't there yet. She must be picking up dinner. "Can you guys eat together before the read-through for the leads? My mom's in town and wanted me to ask you and Portia to come. Sewing projects distracted me or I would've asked earlier."

Owen glanced at his phone. "No worries. We all eat together every night, so … Anyway, Portia will be here soon." Owen was already out of his truck and around to Claire's side, helping her down to the running board of the tall vehicle. "Where do you want to check first?"

"You heard Lulu, the sounds were from the roof."

"Got a ladder?" Owen headed toward the gate to the back yard. "I'll climb up."

Ladder located, Claire followed him up onto the roof. It had a fairly steep pitch. "Wish we'd brought crampons for this."

"Totally. It's a little slippery, too."

"Be careful. Don't slide off. The last thing the town Christmas play needs is to lose another Nicholas by ambulance."

Owen reached the peak and turned to give Claire a hand-up. Their gloves slid apart, slick from the snow. In a trice, Owen whipped his off, offering Claire his bare hand. She pulled hers off and took it. His hand was hot. It sent a surge of warmth through her, as though she'd just flipped on an instant electric blanket.

"Thanks." She had to keep hold of it, but the heat was going to be a problem unless she put it out of her mind. How did he warm her that much? Was he secretly one of those sci-fi mutants with flame-skin?

"Look." Owen nodded in the direction of the far slope of the roof. "Footprints," he whispered.

Instinct made Claire grip Owen's hand for dear life. "Human or animal?"

"Unless animals wear size thirteen boots, you've got a trespassing situation."

Chapter 10

Owen

Owen didn't like it. Not one bit. "Stay here." He shouldn't have commanded Claire, but this was serious. "Don't move."

He crept forward on the ridgepole of the roof of Claire's family's historic two-story brick house. Someone had definitely been up here recently—since the last snow, which, in this time of year in Sugarplum Falls would have to mean within the past twenty-four hours. Owen traced the direction of the prints toward the chimney. At the chimney, they stopped, though.

Had the intruder slipped? Fallen off the roof to his doom? Owen peered at the multiple lines of tracks, but there was no indication of a human-sliding trail from here on down. The rest of the snow looked undisturbed. He couldn't have jumped from here. Or flown.

"If there were also deer hoof-prints, I'd say Santa came early to the old Downing place." The disobedient but brave Claire was at his side. "A Christmas visitor—isn't that the original title of ''Twas the Night Before Christmas' by Clement Moore?"

"It's 'A Visit from St. Nicholas,' I think." But Owen couldn't comment anymore because muffled cries were coming from somewhere nearby. "Shh. Listen."

Claire's eyes flew wide, and she gulped visibly. She'd had to take off her warm gloves at Owen's insistence and was now a frostbite candidate, but worse, he'd brought her up on this slick roof, possibly into contact with some kind of home-invasion creeper.

Not his finest hour as a protector. His mother would chew him out if she knew.

"Is someone there?" Claire hollered. Well, she wasn't cowed by the weirdness.

"Mmmrbbrfffth," came the reply.

Owen tilted his ear. "It's coming from the chimney."

Slip-sliding along, they scrambled together to the chimney stack. Owen peered over the far side, and Claire the near.

"Mmmrbbrfffth!" It came again. It sounded like, "Get me out of here!"

A man was wedged, head-down, in the chimney. Oh, geez. That couldn't be comfortable. In fact, it could be deadly. Yikes!

Alarm filled Claire's voice. "You start pulling him up. I'm calling 911?"

"The police?"

"The ambulance."

"Of course. Okay, I'm on it." Owen wrapped his grip around the guy's ankles. Sure enough, the soles of his boots matched the footprints in the snow on her rooftop. "This is your intruder, Claire." Owen hoisted and lifted for all he was worth. Too bad the fellow was a hulk, since Owen had to heft him a few inches at a time.

"The chimney!" Finished with the emergency call, Claire came to throw her strength into the project, too. "It's wobbling. We have to get him out fast. Adding loose bricks won't help."

With Claire's help, they yanked the guy upward and out of the narrow flue, and Owen set him on the ridgepole, making sure he was steady enough not to go toppling to the ground. Speaking of things that wouldn't help.

"Man, if you guys hadn't come along, I would've died. You know that?" He looked about twenty years old, possibly younger. Soot was smeared over his skin, and the blood had all rushed to his head after several hours hanging like a bat upside down. It was a wonder he hadn't expired. "Thanks. I was able to get out after only a few minutes when I climbed in feet-first last night, but today, I tried going headfirst. Tactical error."

No kidding. Owen looked him over but didn't recognize the wiry guy. He was younger by quite a few years, and dirty. Obviously.

He shook himself, as if to clear his vision. "Claire?" His eyes lit up. "It's you!"

"Me?" Claire looked back and forth before settling her gaze back on the intruder. "Do I know you?"

The guy grimaced. "I forget that I'm the one who knows you and not the other way around." With a sigh, he went on. "It was stupid, trying to meet you this way. I don't know what I was thinking. It's just I've always noticed you, and then I saw you in that picture online with this guy"—he aimed a thumb at Owen—"and I hated what everyone was saying about you stealing your best friend's boyfriend, and I wanted to meet you and do something about it. Give you some cover or something."

Owen could've throttled him. Sliding down the chimney of a girl's house as a get-to-know-you tactic? *Hereby let it be known—don't try this at home, boys. It won't work. And you might die.*

"What if I'd come home and put a fire in the grate while you were stuck?" She looked genuinely concerned for the weirdo, when she should've been more concerned for herself. "What's your name?"

No. They should not exchange names. Only the police should be taking names—for the home invasion booking sheet.

"Rex. Rex Peters." The guy sighed heavily. "I know, I know, I thought none of this through."

"Peters? As in Poppy Peters's brother? The woman who owns The Cider Press downtown?" Owen asked.

Rex gave a shallow nod, pulling his neck backward and grimacing again. "Please don't tell Poppy. She'll kill me. She'll tell all the Kingston family and all the Peters family and I'll be the butt of every joke at the family Christmas ice skating party next week." He turned to Claire. "I, uh, actually came here to ask you to be my date for that. Would you?"

Just then, the ambulance and a police car rolled up, and EMTs took Rex Peters and his badly timed date requests away.

When the commotion died down, just the two of them remained. Owen and Claire stood on solid, frozen ground in the light of the sinking afternoon sun. "You're not going with Rex to the Peters family ice skating party, are you?"

Claire lifted one shoulder. "I don't know. If it's not during play practice, I might."

"What?" Owen stiffened. "Are you being serious? The guy's a stalker!"

"An admirer."

"Semantics won't change the fact he climbed on your roof in the night and tried to enter your home illegally and nearly got himself killed."

"If I were to press charges on that, I can just see the headlines." Claire gave a jovial laugh. "'Santa Claus in Love Gets Thirty Days in Jail.'"

"Fine." When she put it that way, it could be kind of lame to try to prosecute the guy. "I'll agree, he didn't seem particularly dangerous."

True, but when Owen had said guys should be lining up to date Claire, he'd envisioned the front door, not the chimney.

"I just hope he didn't incur any permanent physical damage to himself."

His original question resurfaced. "So, you'd actually consider going out with the guy?" Why the thought irritated him so much, he didn't want to explore.

"Claire is going out with someone?" Portia picked her way toward them, across the well-stomped snow of the yard. Where had Portia been all this time? She'd texted that she'd be right over to help investigate the mystery, but it'd been well over an hour since then. "Who is it? Someone we know?"

Owen leaped to answer. "Rex Peters, and she's not going out with him. Even though he dove down her chimney."

"Let's go inside." Claire led the way and then took on the task of explaining Rex and his heartthrob mistake, as well as put a kettle of water on the stove for hot cocoa.

"Oh, Claire!" Portia put her hand on her heart. "That is the sweetest, most romantic thing ever."

Claire rolled her eyes and dug in the cupboards for plates and forks.

"Maybe, but"—Owen frowned—"she's still not going ice skating with him. He could have died."

"Speaking of died," Portia chortled. "You're the murderer of love, Owen."

"My mom did ask me to try something new," Claire went to open the door, which was rattling.

Owen followed on her heels. "Claire. I'm pretty sure she didn't mean accepting dates with people with no better sense than that."

Claire threw the door wide, and her mom bustled in with packages and bags, which she set on the countertops.

"Hello, all." She hugged Portia and Claire, shook Owen's hand. "I hope you're all really hungry."

They put dinner on the table, and everyone settled in. It was all going fine until partway through the meal when Mrs. Downing—make that Mrs. Edwards now—passed the dish of fried chicken from the grocery store deli to Owen and pointed out the elephant in the room.

"So, what's this like for you, Owen? Dating Portia off-stage but together with Claire on?" She took a big bite of chicken. "You seem to be handling it gracefully, I must say."

"Mom!" Claire must have kicked her mom under the table, because her mom emitted a loud *ow!* and bent over to grab her shin.

"Aw, there's enough of Owen for both of us." Portia placed a hand on Owen's leg beneath the table and waved the awkwardness away like steam with her other hand. "It's show business. People in the dramatic arts aren't squeamish about things like that since they see each other *naked* in the dressing rooms all the time. It's not like a little kissing between my boyfriend and my best friend is going to bother me."

It wouldn't? Owen's chicken leg stopped halfway between his plate and his face, and his jaw might have been hanging open.

"What is it, Owen? Did I shock you?"

No, not much of what Portia said shocked him after a year of dating her. She was lively and unpredictable, which was what had initially hooked him on her. Instead, the realization that there was an onstage kiss coming at him hit like a ton of bricks. "I'm just concerned about Claire is all."

Claire's mom didn't miss a beat. "Oh, don't worry about Claire. She has plenty of experience kissing men, right, dear?"

"Mom, please." Claire colored and turned to Owen.

"Either way, you two had better practice up," Portia declared, taking a sip from her water glass. "A stage-kiss is not something you want to go into unprepared. Trust me. A bad stage-kiss is very difficult to live down."

"Portia, Mrs. Edwards, I don't think—" Owen's gaze slipped to Claire, who looked about the same color as the cranberry drink in her glass. "I think we're embarrassing Claire."

"Oh, please. Claire can handle the teasing." Portia waved her chicken wing in the air beside her temple. "But seriously? It's up to *us* to keep the Sugarplum Falls town Christmas play from being as horrifyingly bad as it has been in the past. So, practice will make perfect."

"Not here or now, though." His teeth clenched while he spoke. "And trust me. Claire and I are going to do it on stage like we've been doing it all our lives."

Now she kicked him under the table. Owen met her eyes, and she mouthed, *double-entendre.*

"Not intended," he said aloud.

"Gosh!" Portia jumped to her feet. "We've got to be there to start the read-through in fifteen. Mom Edwards, can you excuse us?" She kissed Mrs. Edwards on both cheeks and the three of them headed to the door. "You'll come see the play, right? It's brand new, so you won't regret it." She went into cute raptures. "I'm telling you, it's good enough now that it could get national notice. People are going to come from Broadway to see us, if it goes as well as Archie expects."

The mention of Archie killed the cuteness. Was it just Owen, or was Portia mentioning Archie a lot?

"Thanks for dinner, Mrs. Edwards." Owen held the door for Claire and Portia. "It was exactly what we needed. How did you know we'd be too busy to cook or even drive through the burger and shake shack tonight?"

"Just a quick question, Claire." She held her daughter back. "Why don't I see your car here, dear? Nothing's wrong with it, I hope. Your stepdad can help, you know. We don't want you walking in the cold."

Claire met Owen's gaze. "Um—" Then she shook her head quickly *no*. She must not want her mom to know about Rex.

"I brought her here from the boutique. We had a few things to check on before the read-through."

Mrs. Edwards's head snapped upward. "Oh? Just the two of you?" Suspicion adorned her gaze. "Not practicing the final scene already are you, dear?"

"Mom, stop. You're as bad as Portia. I'll kiss Owen on stage and that's it. Maybe hidden behind a hat, and our lips won't even meet."

Something dropped in Owen's gut. Something he shouldn't examine.

"See? Like this." Claire air-kissed her mom goodbye for a demo. "Thanks for making the trip to see me and get a dress and bring us dinner. I really am glad to see you. I miss you tons." Now, she hugged her mom in earnest, and it was time for the read-through.

In the driveway, Claire looked sheepish. "I left my car down at Apple Blossom Boutique."

"You can ride with me," Portia said. "But can Owen take you home? I have a late-night rehearsal with Archie."

"Just the two of you?" He tried loosening his clenched teeth.

"Yeah, he says we need to get the finer points of my character down before the full cast meets tomorrow. I want to be on point, so no one has to wait for me. Everyone's time is precious. I want to be a consummate professional."

Very considerate—if unsettling for her boyfriend. Wasn't spending *more* one-on-one time with his girlfriend the whole point of getting Portia to stay in Sugarplum Falls for the holidays, and for being with her in the play every day? *How's that working out for me?* He glanced at Claire, who shifted her weight and looked at her shoes, like she felt like a third wheel here. Oh, right. She was waiting for his answer.

"I'd be glad to take Claire home after."

"Or, just back to my car," she amended. "Or I could walk. The Kingston Theater isn't that far from Apple Blossom Boutique."

She was not going to walk. Alone? At night? Even in Sugarplum Falls it wasn't a great idea, not with known stalkers about.

"Don't worry, Claire. I've got you." Owen reached for and touched her hand to reassure her, but she met his gaze with their *is that a double-entendre* question in her eye.

Chapter 11

Claire

I've got you. Owen's words reverberated in the night air. Then, they resounded in an echo chamber of Claire's chest cavity during the cast read-through around Archie's kitchen table. *I've got you. I've got you. I've got you.*

The truth was, he'd definitely had her on that roof when he acted like a champion weightlifter and pulled Rex Peters from that literally tight situation—with only Claire's help. Rex Peters must weigh two hundred pounds! And yet Owen Kingston, Clark Kent impersonator, had extracted the guy like Rex was a five-year-old.

While that act should not stir feelings beyond gratitude, for some reason, all evening it had been *I've got you* on a loop.

I felt so protected.

Ever since Dad left, Claire had longed to feel protected. Mom had done her best, but there had been so many periods of scarcity, of uncertainty about what the next day would bring—or what it wouldn't bring, physically and emotionally.

Yes, there'd been the empty refrigerator days now and then, but also empty Claire days. As the middle child, Claire had placed herself as buffer between Taylor and Bailee in their arguments. When Claire couldn't stop the fights, she let the sisters turn on her to distract them from each other. Mom hadn't stepped in.

Maybe Mom hadn't noticed.

Mom came today, though. She's definitely trying now. And luckily, she'd made it through the pass prior to the avalanche.

"Claire, are you still planning on playing Caroline for us?" Archie asked. Claire looked up from the blur of words on her script to find all eyes on her. "It's your cue."

"Geez. Sorry. What scene are we on?" She shifted in her folding chair in the circle.

Portia mouthed the words, *professionalism, please.* Then she double blinked to show she was joking. "Page sixteen."

Gently, Owen reached over to the pages on Claire's lap and turned three sheets of paper and pointed to Claire's line. "Here," he whispered. "It's just you and me in this scene."

"Haven't you even read through the script yet?" Donny Gatwick asked.

Of course she had, but she hadn't memorized anything yet. "Sorry, I've been sewing costumes."

"Sure, you have. With Santa Claus." A snicker erupted from around the circle at Marie Gatwick's chortling. "I'm friends with Rex Peters. I know what you've been doing."

"I heard it on my police scanner," a different cast member chimed in. "Rex is fine, by the way, in case you care, Claire."

She did care. Of course she cared. "I'm so glad to hear that."

More snickers.

Archie tried to regain control of the room, but whispers erupted and hands covered mouths while the information went around like that game, gossip. "Guys. Let's keep going. Claire, you'll keep your eyes on the script, right? You're Caroline. We need you to take this seriously."

"Everyone." The legs of Owen's chair scraped across the wood planks of the kitchen floor, and he stood up, looking really ticked off. "Leave her alone. Unless one of you has the sewing skills to step up and help her finish all ten dozen costume pieces she's been tasked to create, zip it. And kindly recall, Claire Downing is doing more for this play than the rest of us put together."

That shut down the rumor mill. Even Archie looked a little cowed.

Claire flushed hot, but she stole a glance at Owen. Fury was draining from his face, and his eyes were trained on his script.

With trepidation, Claire read her line. "When church bells ring, I always think of Christmas. And when I think of Christmas, I think of you, Nicholas— and your younger brother."

In this newer version of the play, Nicholas and Caroline had to work together to help Nicholas heal from the past, where he'd lost a younger brother into the ice of Lake Sugar. Yeah, it had a lot more punch than the original town Christmas play. It even had the potential to jerk a few tears from the audience.

Archie pushed the cast onward, and they finally made it to the end of the play. "Did you like it? What do you think? Can we make this town love Christmas again?"

Had Sugarplum Falls ever *not* loved Christmas? Perish the thought. But the cast leads—all dozen of them—assented that they could, indeed, renew the Christmas Spirit in Sugarplum Falls with this rendition.

Everyone dispersed to get soda and cookies from the refreshments table.

"It's definitely an upgrade from the old version." Owen brought Claire a glass of ginger ale with two ice cubes. "We might be out of our acting depth."

"No matter what, that would be true of me." Claire stared into her drink. "Thanks for that, back there."

The ice cubes in Owen's glass clinked. "I've been thinking about what Portia said."

Oh, no. Which thing? Claire followed him into a corner of the living room where no one else was talking. They stood near the Christmas tree, which had lights but no decorations. "Keep in mind, Portia tends to say a lot of things."

"I can sense that. But what I mean is about the kiss."

Claire froze. Suddenly, her gaze was a laser pointer on Owen's mouth. Full lower lip, looking slightly in need of ChapStick. Upper lip with a perfect cupid's bow. Had they always looked so tempting?

Claire gulped. "Um, what about it?" She stared on, couldn't tear her eyes off his mouth. Now his lips had slightly parted, and he took a sip of ginger ale, leaving a tiny, gleaming gold bead of moisture in the center of the bottom one.

A hiccup erupted at the back of her throat, and she bobbled her ginger ale. Some splashed on the back of her hand.

"Are you okay?" Owen reached for a napkin and patted at the spill. "Something wrong?"

Claire stared at how he gently removed the drops from her skin.

Uh-oh. She was feeling all the wrong things right now.

"Nope. I'm fine." It was Claire's body chemistry that was saying all the wrong things. "Nothing's wrong."

Lies! Terrible lies! She'd been ogling her bestie's boyfriend's kisser. Not fine. In any sense.

"Uh, so. About the kiss."

If she were a puppy dog, she would've been panting, ready to lick his face. "Can we talk about it later? Or maybe you should text me your thoughts on this."

"It's totally uncomfortable, right?"

"Way." Now, at last she could rip her gaze from his mouth and look him in the eye. In them, worry and tenderness were at war. "I think maybe Portia is underestimating me." As in Claire's emotions—feelings that might awaken between friends, or at least on Claire's side, if she were suddenly to kiss Owen Kingston.

Meaning, emotions like guilt, self-loathing, and so forth.

Is lust an emotion? 'Cause if so, it was wide awake a second ago.

She'd better sing it a good lullaby starting this second.

"I meant the practicing part. There's no way we are going to be able to watch ourselves kiss and know whether it's stage-ready. We could—I don't know—film it, but that seems ..."

"Kinky." She finished the sentence for him, and he winced. "I agree, Owen. Well, if we ask her to, I'm sure Portia will be an objective observer and give us her unvarnished opinion."

"She's full of those." He gave a merry huff-laugh. "One thing you can count on in life. No varnish from Portia." Then, a half-smile spread across his face, the one he often wore when he was speaking of Portia Sutherland. "What you see is what you get."

"You like that about her." Claire couldn't agree more. Nothing but Portia's acting was a façade. "It's made for a good friendship. She isn't a backstabber. She never gossips about me. Sure, she does crazy, thoughtless stunts like pops pictures of you and me up on social media without considering consequences, and she makes me go with her to sit on the department store Santa's lap and then offer him our phone number, and any number of other cringe-worthy things, but she is all good intentions—like doing anything and everything to promote the new and improved town Christmas play."

"You nailed it. She'll do anything and everything." Owen nodded staring down into his near-empty soda glass, but the little half-smile wasn't there anymore. "So, yeah. I'll see if she can be our kiss-judge, or director, or coach." His head popped upward. "Not that I need any direction in the kissing department. I'm practically officially certified." His brow raised.

"Oh, I believe you." Claire's traitorous stare fixed itself on his upper lip again. It had such definition, almost a little dark red line at the edge. And this time of day, that swarthy hint of stubble above it might prickle against a girl lucky enough to take coaching from the guy.

So masculine.

Oh, my gosh! A swift intake of breath, and Claire whirled around and stalked away from the mind-melting sight. That guy! Who did he think he was? And Portia! How could she put Claire in a situation where she'd be forced to kiss Owen? When Owen clearly loved Portia—and would do anything for her.

Anything. Including kissing Claire. When it meant nothing to him. And was starting to possibly mean something to Claire.

I've always liked Owen. I just never for a second hoped he might see me as someone he could ... you know. Kiss.

She gulped. And then gulped again. The lump in her throat went nowhere.

"Claire, wait. Where are you going?" Owen caught up to her, catching her elbow.

"I'd, uh, better get back to the costumes. I'm desperately behind." She yanked free and walked fast toward the front door, not even putting on her coat, just stepping out into the bitter-cold wind of the Sugarplum Falls December night.

But Owen was at her heels. "Wait, Claire. I'm supposed to drive you back to your shop, remember?"

Oh, right. Shoot. "I'll walk." Pile up the lies—since Archie lived on the posh side of the Sugar River Bridge, with all the mansions, a good three-mile walk in the cold from Orchard Street. "See you at rehearsal tomorrow."

"Claire!" Owen jogged and easily caught up with her. He caught her by the elbow. "Hey, slow down. You shouldn't walk alone at night. Not when there are … stalkers."

"Rex Peters hardly qualifies as a stalker. Weird, maybe. Stalker, no."

"I'll drive you to the shop, anyway." Owen steered her toward his truck.

A rectangle of light striped across the driveway. "Guys! Oh, good." Portia jogged toward them, wrapping her neck with a scarf. "I'm glad you're still here." She was breathing hard. "I—I can't let this go on."

Claire's blood chilled. *Portia saw my wanton gaze at Owen's mouth. I knew it!* "Portia, I can explain."

But Portia was talking over her. "That whole Rex Peters thing has me freaked out."

Rex Peters! "Why? He tried sliding down my house's chimney flue, not yours."

"It's dangerous. He might be like those bugs."

"Bugs?" Claire asked. Portia was anything but expected.

"What are you talking about?" Owen dropped his hand from Claire's back. "I mean, I don't relish the idea of Rex Peters chasing Claire any more than you do, but—"

"My best friend in the world is under attack." Portia stomped her boot. "And it's my fault. If I hadn't posted that photo, none of this would have happened."

Totally true. Neither Claire nor Owen put up an argument.

"So, bugs!" Portia waited for their reaction and got none. "I mean—if there's one lovesick admirer making rash advances, then there are bound to be more."

Snort. Claire pushed Owen aside and climbed onto the truck's seat. "Much as I'd love to believe that the men of Sugarplum Falls are secretly in love with me and would do anything to get near me, it's just not the case."

"Hear me out." Portia clung to Claire's wrist, but she pulled it inside the truck.

"Good night, guys. I need to head back to the sewing."

"I'll make sure you get there safely." Owen started pressing the door closed, but Portia wedged herself into the way.

"See? This is what I'm getting at." Portia waved her hand between Claire and Owen. "Owen, you get it, right? The fact that Claire needs a bodyguard to move into her house and protect her at all times?"

Chapter 12

Owen

I t was one thing to date a woman who was full of surprises. It was an entirely different thing to date a woman who yanked the rug out from underfoot and toppled a guy to the ground.

"Bodyguard?" Owen stuttered, nearly choking on the word. "Move into Claire's house?"

"Of course! What other solution is there?" Portia planted her feet like they'd grown apple tree roots. "Claire's my bestie. She's all alone in that big house at the end of that road. Who would hear her if she screamed?"

Nice visual. Geez.

Beside them, Claire did choke out a muffled scream. "I can take care of myself."

"I insist." Portia pulled Claire into a hug. "You are the one who has said how much you can't bear being alone so often. I don't want that for you, Claire. We're here for you, Owen and I—in everything. This is perfect for Owen, since he's been complaining about needing to replace his carpet."

Claire turned to him, beet red. Whether with anger or embarrassment, it wasn't clear. Her mouth opened and closed several times, like a fish that jumped out of the tank.

"Claire, this isn't my idea."

Portia interrupted. "Owen, you know this would be a perfect opportunity to hire that out—and in the meantime spend the night with Claire."

With a panic-laced *double-entendre* question in her eye, Claire met Owen's gaze. "It's not necessary." It came out like meat through a grinder.

"Nope. Not a good idea." Owen wiped his palms together as if brushing off dirt. "If I'm going to be doing the play and the sets, adding home improvement, too? No way."

"I'm walking to my boutique." Claire hopped out of the truck and started walking down the driveway. "No one is moving in with me. In fact, since I'll be at the shop all hours of the day and night, the point is moot. See you later."

Owen was torn. Go after her, or face Portia and get rid of this terrible plan.

"Bye, love," Portia called. "See you tomorrow. I'll stop by the shop to talk about the angel costume." She turned back to Owen. "About the carpet removal, be rational. You wouldn't be doing it yourself." She fanned her face with the fringe of her scarf. "What better time to rescue a friend in need? This way, she doesn't feel like she's being a bother. She's helping *you* out. It's mutually beneficial. For a *friend*."

A friend I'm supposed to kiss. And live with. A female friend. An attractive, strawberry blonde female friend with long legs and an incredible sense of exactly what I need to heal my family.

"Please? For my peace of mind?" Portia looked even more strikingly pretty when she was helping people and arranging their lives. And it was great that she felt so protective of Claire. It was sweet. "For me?"

Nevertheless ... "I'm not moving in with Claire."

"It's for her safety. Who else saw the photo?"

"Don't you know how inappropriate that would look? Rex's home invasion was to protect her from haters. If I move in, it triggers more haters who love you." Okay, and fine, from women who had their sights trained on Owen and were jealous of anyone he paid attention to.

"You spend half your time at Claire's house with me already. Please?" Portia batted her lashes. "It's not like you'd be doing anything other than the kissing practice you need for the play. Which, by the way—the answer is yes. I'll be glad to coach you two on your stage kisses. Once you've done a few practice runs in private. I know Claire, okay? She's not going to want an audience during the dry run."

"You—? You'll what?" How did Portia even know?

She sniff-laughed. "Don't look so alarmed. Donny and Marie overheard you guys talking at the refreshment table and told me you'll need a coach and you chose me. *Thank you!* I accept." She pressed a kiss to his cheek, dry and cool.

Geez. First the kissing, now the moving in. What was Portia trying to do to him? To *them*? As a couple? And worse, to Claire? Because Claire was the true innocent victim of Portia's whim-a-thon.

"Hear me out on this. Logically, okay?" He took a steadying breath. "I can't move in with and kiss my girlfriend's best friend, Portia." He held these truths to be self-evident. Couldn't she, as well? "It goes against my every grain."

"Is it the *she's my girlfriend's best friend* part?" Portia looked at her nails. "Because that's easy to remedy."

A roaring sounded in his ears, hooves of the four horsemen of the apocalypse. "How?" Owen's own voice was difficult to hear over the thundering hooves of impending change. "You cannot drop Claire as your best friend." Claire was already far too-often overlooked and left out. "Not even temporarily. It's Christmas, and she's done so much for this play, and—"

Portia whacked him with the tips of her scarf. "Not her, silly. You."

Him? "Me?" All the horses stopped. His whole brain went silent. Like the deafness after a bombshell explodes.

"Just like you said, temporarily. Until the play is over."

"Temporarily." It sank in. She was dumping him. "Break up—for the play?" All his efforts to keep her in town were definitely not having the intended effect. His back fell against the side of his truck. "This is not how I saw this conversation going."

With a seductive bat of her eyelashes, Portia fell against his chest and wrapped her arms around him. "Oh, Owen. This isn't for me, it's for your conscience. Don't you know how much I care about your conscience? It's a very big part of you. A huge part of what I admire about you. You're so *good*."

93

One thing was for sure, he didn't *feel* good. He felt like a guy getting the heave-ho. "We're not going to break up."

"Actually, the way I understand it, a break-up isn't often a mutual decision. In fact, it's usually rather one-sided. And tonight, I am the side who is telling you we're through—until the end of the play—so that you can happily, and *ethically*, kiss Claire Downing to your heart's content, and so you can move into her house and keep her safe. Then, when it's all over, whoosh! We'll get back together again and it'll be like nothing has changed." She pulled one of those smiles at him like she'd just laid out a plan for world peace forevermore. "It's because of my love for both of you. I'm the one sacrificing here."

It didn't sound that way. Or feel that way. Owen's heart was on the altar, being burned over and over again.

"Portia, *no,*" he whispered, hoarse and almost afraid. "This isn't why I took on the play. I did it to be together. With you."

"And you will be. When it's over."

Her horrible plan took him giant strides away from the whole point of spending more time with her to see if they were compatible and a good fit for marriage. It took him away from Portia, period, and thrust him—literally—into Claire's arms.

"Listen, and listen well. I'm not letting you break up with me. We'll figure out something else." Could someone else play the part of Nicholas? Could he find an out-of-town actor to play that part, and—

No. It'd end up being someone like Fletch. Or worse. Claire deserved better. If only one of his cousins could step in, take up the role. Except, they couldn't. Or wouldn't. Even if Owen explained that it was the best way to keep Portia. *If I tell them that, they'll just laugh.* The Kingstons hadn't necessarily fallen in love with Portia the way Owen had. They'd probably tell him to date Claire.

"I can see the wheels turning in your mind. You're coming around to my brilliant plan, aren't you? Kiss me to tell me you're on board with this."

Owen tilted his head forward to kiss her, not yet decided about the *on board* thing. His lips were cold, and hers were inviting, and she was only doing this for his sake, right?

"Portia!" The front door flung open. "There you are!" Archie huffed and his breath made a huge cloud of white. "I've been looking all over the house for you. Are you ready for the coaching session?"

The special coaching session with Archie, one on one. Should Owen punch the guy?

Play the long game, dude. The long game excludes punching out the director of the play that is your girlfriend's dream job with a starring role.

Make that ex-girlfriend.

Oh, to rewind the past twenty minutes.

"Having a good night, Kingston?" Archie raised a brow. "Where's our Caroline? Aren't you taking care of her?"

Claire was walking. In the night. Shoot.

"Sorry to be late, Arch!" Portia bounced toward the man in the cardigan. "I was just saying goodbye to my ex-boyfriend." She gave an exaggerated wink over her shoulder at Owen, one that made an unfamiliar sickness slosh inside him. "So, yeah. We're good to rehearse."

"Ex-boyfriend?" A ripple of excitement and delight rippled over Archie's countenance, curse him. "You're not together?"

"Yes, we are," Owen asserted.

But not loudly enough to be heard over Portia's, "We're on a break." Then, she turned and blew Owen a kiss. "I'll miss you. It's been fun while it lasted. Maybe it can be fun again." Another wink. "Meanwhile, let your current fun be had by kissing my best friend."

Slosh. His stomach literally sloshed as Portia and Archie disappeared into the house, and the door closed behind them, taking with it the stripe of golden light from inside.

Owen stood in the dark of Archie's driveway, with only a distant streetlight and the cold blue light of stars above.

What just happened? And why did he feel so awful?

Snow sprinkled from above, dotting his cheeks and forehead, chilling him through. He could've stood there until he became a snowman, a tragic figure.

But—no. He was Owen Kingston, even though he'd never felt less like

95

himself in his life. With effort, he yanked his boots from where they'd frozen to the spot and got inside his truck. He drove along, looking for Claire.

Just as he passed the Apple Blossom Boutique, she was standing at the door unlocking it. Some kind Sugarplum Fallsian must have given her a ride.

She went safely inside. Safe—for now.

His head hurt so much.

Instead of going back to his house, which—Portia was right—did need the carpet replaced, he steered along Orchard Street all the way to its namesake destination on the foothills side of Sugarplum Falls.

Aw, man. Someone had already pulled the plug on the playground for the night. No orchard lights for Owen.

He stomped across the parking lot of the kids' area, finally taking out his phone to serve as a flashlight after he caught his foot on a stray garden hose that should've been put away before snow fell. *Dang it.* The light helped, and soon he'd made his way to the tool shed. It wasn't locked, so once inside he found the outlet and flipped the amperage switch.

Light flooded his world.

Well, mostly. It was more like a mini-flood.

Outside, he made a slow trek around the perimeter, keeping near the trees, which shed light in white, green, and red. This year, the crew had done a great job getting lights on practically every branch and twig. The effect was stunning.

However, Claire wasn't wrong—there could be more. Lots more. Instead of a single row of trees nearest the sandy area ablaze with lights, there could be row after row in concentric circles. Or—no. It could be an extended walk, up the path through the apricots toward the apples and beyond that to the cherries. Of course, lighting every tree on the acreage would be way beyond the scope of possibility.

Still, an amble along the trails where Granddad walked through the different areas of Kingston Orchards, with lights blazing on every branch lining the trail, could be just the perfect thing. Claire's sweet idea.

On a night like tonight, when everything seems to go sideways, it'd sure help me to have a little more light.

"Owen? Is that you?" A female voice cut the darkness. Mom's. "I saw a truck like yours as I was heading home, and I stopped to unplug the Orchard Walk lights. Someone left them on."

"Yeah, it's me, Mom." Owen briefly shone his flashlight on his face and smiled. "I didn't mean to scare you. I'm the one who plugged them back in. Don't think an orchard worker forgot."

"Weren't you at a play practice tonight? How is that going? I heard Portia didn't get the Caroline part, and Claire did. Is that ... going all right?"

No. Not all right at all.

"From your silence, I'll take that it's awkward."

"A lot less awkward than it had been three hours ago. And a lot more, at the same time. Never mind that. Anyway, to answer your question, it's the town Christmas play, so it's pretty much what you'd expect."

"Marie Gatwick told me tonight that the theater had flooded, causing a lot of damage to the props and things. How awful. But Archie Holdaway was willing to take on the task anyway. Good for him."

Yeah. Good for Archie. The guy who'd insisted on *special coaching sessions* with Portia tonight. Punching him out still wasn't a good idea an hour later.

"I'm remaking the sets, and Claire is redoing all the costumes."

"All of them! But I hear the cast size tripled. How on earth can she possibly?" Mom was gasping. "I mean, I do a lot of quilting, so I know my way around a sewing machine, but she must be superhuman if she's getting all of them done in that amount of time. Did she close her boutique?"

No, she hadn't. Claire was burning the midnight oil. "I think she's managing."

"Son. I know you think the world of her, and that your faith in her is implicit, but ..." Mom shuddered. "Anyway, I guess I'll ask what I came to find out in the first place. What are you doing out here in the night?"

How much should he tell her? Certainly not about the breakup. It was temporary. The Kingston family might get the wrong idea about Portia and misunderstand her noble notions. "I was thinking about the family and the orchard and Granddad. It's been a rough year."

97

"You can say that again." Mom's wistfulness extended to Dad, of course. And to the accident Owen had caused that doubly complicated the year. Or triply. More. "We might not even schedule the annual sledding and doughnuts day again. Everyone is on edge. I'm sure you've noticed."

He'd been steeping himself in it, not merely noticing. "What would you think of a family project to bring us together?"

"That depends on what it is." Mom was usually one to proceed with caution. "Go on. Tell me your idea."

"To preface, it's not my idea. It's Claire's." Owen explained the scheme—in a nutshell.

Never in his life had Owen seen a greater transformation on Mom's countenance. She'd gone from her daily pulled-lines-of-stressed-caregiver look to soft and hopeful.

For the first time in months.

"Oh, son. It would have pleased your Granddad to no end. And your dad will love it!"

"You think?" But Dad? He wouldn't be aware of it. "Then, I should go ahead?"

Mom hugged him, long and hard. "Tell Claire thank you." She pressed a chilly kiss to his cheek and hurried off toward her car, a spring in her step.

So, it was happening. Wow.

I can't wait to tell Claire! Owen whipped out his phone to give her the news. Sure, it was past midnight now, but she was still sewing. She had to be up. He called up her contact.

Instead of hitting *text,* however, his thumb pressed the *dial* button.

Gaffe! Suddenly he was calling her in the middle of the night? Geez. Push as he might to get the call to hang up, the skin on the pads of his fingers was too cold. The screen wouldn't register his touch. He blew on them and tried again, but—

"Hello? Owen? Is everything okay?"

Geez. "Yeah. I—" Didn't mean to call? Ugh. It would sound like he'd been staring at her contact number on the screen, contemplating it.

"I heard."

"Heard what?" About the Orchard Walk idea? Already? Was she clairvoyant? "Isn't it great news? I think it's really going to make things better in my family."

"Really? They didn't like her? Everyone likes her. She's Portia."

The brain-dominoes fell into place, ending with an arrow pointing at the breakup. Who'd told Claire? And what did she know about the temporary situation? He'd tackle that in daylight.

"Sorry. I actually called to tell you I'm taking your suggestion to catalyze a Kingston family project and add ten million lights to the orchard in honor of my granddad. I thought you'd want to know."

For a second there was a pause. Uh-oh. Had he awakened Claire with his phone call, and she'd fallen back to sleep while he effervesced about his plan?

Who am I? Calling women in the night? Women I'm not dating. Owen Kingston does not call women in the night with news.

But ... he could become that guy. Now that he was a single man. He could be dating practically anyone at this point. Claire included, other than she was Portia's best friend, which was verboten in almost every way.

Never mind the awkwardness of everything else that happened this evening.

"That's great," Claire answered at last. "I'm sure it will help your family a lot, like you said."

And now he saw how his earlier statement must have sounded—like the Kingston family wasn't too keen on Portia Sutherland. Come on, Odessa had married Portia's cousin Heath. The Kingstons and the Sutherlands were of one mind and one heart when it came to dedication to Sugarplum Falls. They had to love her, if only for her family connections.

"Yeah, that's what I really hope. So, I wanted to say thanks for the idea."

"Of course." Claire paused again. "But Owen? Portia called to explain. Are you ... okay?"

"I'm fine." Sort of. He wasn't himself, but otherwise, he was all right. Vertical, breathing, able to think coherent thoughts about the future of the Kingston family. That was fine enough, considering his girlfriend deemed their relationship a lower priority than that of a town Christmas play. "I know she did it with the intent that I'd move in with you—"

"That can't happen. I made that abundantly clear to her."

Whew. At least Claire could make things clear to Portia, if no one else could. "Good."

"Right?" Claire exhaled. "I'm glad that's not your intent."

See? Claire had her head on straight. Unlike him, she wasn't thinking about their possibility of dating just because he'd been rendered single. "Well, good night." Wait—had she gone home? "Are you still sewing?"

"Probably only for another hour. I've pulled some late nights recently. If I don't sleep at all, I've found, my seams go catawampus."

"Then you're going home?"

Claire heaved a loud sigh. "Seriously, Owen. I don't need someone to come to my house. Rex is not going to attack in the night. It's fine. But I will say I'm glad you called to let me know about your orchard plan. It'll be nice to have somewhere to go and feel the light."

Feel? Not *see*?

Except, no. The light was something Owen had been missing tonight, and he'd been feeling all that darkness. Coming to the orchard and turning on the lights definitely had been a feeling, much more than a sight.

Claire, right again.

"Thanks, Claire. I'll see you tomorrow at the rehearsal." And every other day of rehearsal. Maybe he shouldn't be looking forward to it as much as he was, but having a reason to see her, to be around her, to *feel her light*, was something Owen couldn't help himself but look forward to.

And yet, I'm supposedly getting back together with Portia after this is all over.

Chapter 13

Claire

It took all Claire's willpower to peel her eyes open, but the sun's glare through her window curtains shouted that morning had come to her house, like it or not.

Rex, however, had not arrived. Neither he nor his squashed form were perched inside her chimney at this time. See? There'd been no call for Owen to come sleep at her house and act as bodyguard.

However, urghlglrgh. He would have to show up later on this afternoon, acting in a different role—as her stage-kiss practice dummy. Unless ... unless they could get out of it! That was it. If they could convince Archie and Portia that the kiss shouldn't be rehearsed—that it wouldn't look fresh enough if they practiced too much—then Claire could keep all herself intact and not have to face up to the feelings that had slammed her right in the hormones the other night on the porch swing, or after the read-through when she'd been mesmerized by the drop of golden ginger ale on Owen's lower lip.

Sigh.

What are we even doing? We're not dating. We're friends. We're mutual friends of Portia. He's her ex, and I'm her best friend, and that makes us ...

Nope. That wasn't right, either. She was too sleep-deprived to define any relationship. She needed a good, cold shot of ginger ale to wake her.

Or a cold shower.

After that, though, she could chase the ginger with a cardamom spice doughnut from Mrs. Toledo at Sugarbabies, and then her brain might work again—in time to concentrate on the kazillion costumes she needed all her faculties to create.

Yup. Up and at 'em.

Later though, as she walked in the back door of the shop, it hit her—her brain might function, but the *world* would not!

Owen and Portia had broken up!

But ... for how long?

Portia had hinted at nothing. Claire placed her palm across her forehead and pressed.

The implications piled one on top of another, like crêpes off the pan on Christmas morning. Without Owen as her anchor to Sugarplum Falls, Portia might float off after any old acting job that called her away. Heartbroken over Portia, Owen might shy away from Claire's life because of sad memories. Make a clean break.

Until last night, Claire had been rich—the possessor of two friends who'd be there for her no matter what. Now, with this change-up, the fabric of Claire's life in Sugarplum Falls went into jeopardy. Blast it! If she weren't so stupidly shy! If only she'd made other friends as a backup plan. If only, if only ...

Piles of cut fabric could suffocate her if she crawled into them and never came out, right?

First, I'll lose Owen, and then I'll lose Portia. Or, would it be the other way around? No matter what, one of those giant, loud analog clocks began to tick an echoing, menacing countdown toward Claire's loss.

"Knock, knock." Lulu stood at the door, a big grin on her face. "You made it!"

Huge heaving sigh. "Sorry I'm late."

"No, I'm sorry you stayed so late. But, thank you for what you did for me yesterday."

"What was that?" Claire tilted her head. Yesterday was ages ago, judging by her emotional clock.

102

"You vindicated me to Eugene! He doesn't think I'm crazy anymore for thinking someone was stuck on your roof and for calling the police. And the police don't either. Thank you. I won't be the town nutcase anymore." Lulu hugged her quickly.

Claire offered a tired—make that exhausted—smile. "Glad to help."

Lulu's smile faded. "What is it, sugar?" She sat down in the chair across from Claire's work station. "You look like someone stole the angel off the top of your Christmas tree."

"A star goes on the top of the tree."

"That's an argument for another day. What's eating you? Is it this pile of costumes you're supposed to sew?"

That, and all the other things. One shoulder up, and *drop*.

"I heard from someone who came in here earlier, Donny Gatwick? He told me what's happening tomorrow night at practice. If that's what is bothering you, I can definitely understand."

The kiss? Oh, garshk. That, too? "That's—it's—" There was no adjective for what it was.

"Less of a big deal now that Portia dumped Owen?" Lulu offered. "Yeah, I had a long conversation with Marie Gatwick. I hope gossip is one of the lower sins. But it wasn't meant with any malice, I promise. All in love and concern."

Uh-huh. The pinching between Claire's eyebrows stabbed hard. "I'm going to get to work on these costumes."

"I'll handle the front of the store, dear. You're going to be great. And I have a good feeling about these costumes, that they'll get done in a breeze."

"A breeze."

"Really! I don't just say that in flattery. I really do have a feeling that—"

The front bells jingled, and Lulu left like a shot to help greet whoever it was. Claire ducked her head over the wool great-coat meant for Mr. Milliken as the play's town mayor. Thick layers, and her fingertips' raw skin snagging on the weave, were not a breeze.

"Knock, knock again?" Lulu interrupted. "Is it okay if I let someone come back here to see you?"

103

"I can meet whoever it is out front." Claire stood, but then, she halted. Behind Lulu was a beaming face. "Mrs. Kingston! Come in." Claire fell back into her chair, seeing as the pile of dark wool for the coat was too heavy to keep standing, and moving it mid-seam was out of the question. "Excuse me for not coming to greet you."

"Are all these bolts of fabric meant to be transformed into costumes for the play?" Owen's mom stepped toward a neatly folded stack of yardage that Claire hadn't even begun to place the patterns on yet for cutting out. "This calico has a nice, understated pattern. It will be nice for the mayor's wife's dress."

How could Mrs. Kingston tell that was its intended purpose? Mind-reader. That had to be it.

"I've got my work not-yet-cut-out-for-me." Grimace. "Is Owen all right?" After Portia's call, Claire hadn't been able to think about anything except Owen's inevitable anguish. "He called me last night, but sounded fine. When did you talk to him last?"

Mrs. Kingston turned around, her arms laden with red velvet, the Santa Claus costume. "This visit isn't about Owen. He's fine. Better than ever, I'd say."

Better than ever! What? "He told you, then?"

"Yes, about the Orchard Walk—that it was your idea. You're an angel. An angel on earth!" Owen's mom beamed streams of glory at Claire. It was easy to see where Owen got his brilliant smile and straight teeth. "Thank you. I think it's going to help everything."

But what about the breakup with Portia? Obviously, Mrs. Kingston didn't know. Claire should not be the one to tell her. "If this visit isn't about Owen, then ...?"

"It's about you."

About Claire! "Don't thank me. Owen's the one who will put it into motion."

"Owen is a wonder, for sure. Meanwhile, you've been in perpetual motion. I can see that." She gave a nod toward the stack of completed costumes. All the townspeople's vests. Every apron for the women. All the newsboy hats. The short trousers for the boys in the play. They were complete. But it was the tip of the iceberg. "Good work. Have you slept? You should—because I'm here to offer my services. No, the services of all the Kingston women."

"But, do you sew?"

"Not as well or as quickly as you do, but eighteen women with medium skill can sew faster than one Wonder Woman."

"Eighteen?" Claire still couldn't extract herself from the heavy wool to stop the freight train of Owen's mom as she gathered up several stacks of fabric.

"Claire. I'm offering the family quilting club's expertise to this project. I assume you've got this mass organized clearly enough that I'll know what to do?"

"The instructions are with each set of cut fabric. The master list is here." Claire leaned out forward and tugged one of her several copies from her inbox. "The checkmarks are the finished pieces."

"My, my. You've done a lot already."

A third, at most. And that was working 'round the clock. "The dress rehearsal is in two weeks."

"Good grief! And I hear you've got a role in the play, too. Plus this shop to run?"

"Lulu is my business partner, and she's the heart of the store. She's managing."

"No, I'm not!" Lulu's voice echoed through the rafters. *Eavesdropper.* Although, the shop allowed for nothing else. After all, Claire had heard every word spoken between Archie and Mayor Lang the other day. "I'm not managing. I'm keeping my head above water, though. Merry Christmas!"

"Well, leave these to me." Mrs. Kingston had a full armload. "And I'll be back for the rest. Of course, you probably have a pet project you'll want to work on. A creative piece. Like that wool greatcoat there. Very nice. Lots of fine detail work involved."

"And Portia's Evangeline costume." Finally, Claire extracted herself from the heavy wool and came to help Mrs. Kingston take the bolts of fabric out to her car.

"Evangeline, huh? That's a new one. I heard there were changes. But yes. I'll leave those trickier tasks to you, while we Kingston Kutters handle the repetitive busy-work."

Could this be real? Or was Claire just dreaming that someone had come to her rescue? "I'd put up an argument, Mrs. Kingston, but I'm frankly too tired. I could absolutely use a big save here." A wobble tinged her voice. She swallowed it down. "Thank you—and thank the Kutters for me. And Owen! Thank Owen, too?"

Mrs. Kingston smiled as if Claire had just said her favorite word. "I'll do that. Now, if you finish the greatcoat and whatever other fancywork costumes that need done, come on down to the farmhouse. We'll all work the remaining costumes together. It'll be fun. You'll like the women."

"Are they all Kingstons?" Claire's breath steamed in the cold outdoors.

"Mostly, but they all feel like family." Mrs. Kingston took her loads of fabric—it required two trips for both of them to get it out to her trunk—and before she left, she paused to give Claire a big, long hug. "Thank you for letting me help. I needed something important to do this Christmas."

Waves of understanding washed through Claire. Mrs. Kingston had had a tough year. She'd lost her father-in-law, the anchor of her extended family, and then had lost—in almost every sense of the word—her husband in quick succession. Serving the community probably would take her mind off the heaviness.

Claire hugged her back, until Mrs. Kingston let go and drove off with the loads of fabric.

As she turned to go inside, Claire ran smack dab into the broad chest of Owen Kingston.

"Was that my mother's car?" He followed her to the door of the shop, but they didn't go inside.

"Yes. She's going to help me with the costumes." And she'd offered to let Claire into her quilting circle. Potential friends! Good glory.

I don't know quite how to react. Elation? Terror? Relief?

"Really? She is?" Owen's mouth dropped wide, but after a second, he

106

closed it again, and murmured *good.*

"I'm so relieved. Thanks for sending her my way."

"I didn't. I just mentioned you were sewing."

"Well, I guess that was enough for her."

"She's a good person. She doesn't get to help in the community much these days. It'll be good for her." He took her hand and started walking away from the shop. "Are you ready for our rehearsal?"

Claire had to replay his words three times before understanding them. Her mental faculties were all firing on one thing: *he's holding my hand!*

And he isn't with Portia anymore.

Chapter 14

Owen

Owen stared at his hand on the steering wheel. It still pulsated from holding Claire's. Something about her touch ...

"Your truck smells like ... garlic?"

"I brought you Mario's. Did you say you have our costumes ready?" What he'd really meant to ask was whether she was ready to practice their stage kiss—offstage. But now, with the way his hand had just felt at her touch, maybe it wasn't such a good idea. "Are they at your boutique with the rest of the costumes?"

"They're at my house."

Even better. "I'd love to not be one of the regular acting types who changes clothes in the theater's dressing room." The lower the chance of strangers walking in as he put on some kind of Victorian getup, the better.

"Same." Claire closed her eyes. "I have no idea how Portia—or anyone— does that." She pulled a little wincing smile. "To be honest, even though we've been friends for a long time, there are a lot of things I don't understand about Portia."

No kidding. Portia had broken up with him—why, exactly?

Except, were they broken up or not?

Not. But yes. Yes. They were.

Claire leaned over and inhaled at the top of the bag. "I love Mario's."

Owen couldn't steer the truck while she was doing that. Eyes closed, and with her strawberry blonde hair falling over her shoulder and framing her face, she looked better than the Italian food smelled. And that was saying something.

"Can you eat a calzone while we drive?" He tore his eyes away and began to drive down Orchard Street toward Claire's place, a route as familiar as to his own house. "Or do you want to wait until we get to your place?"

"I can eat a Mario's calzone while I'm standing on my head. Underwater." She pulled the food from the bag and unwrapped a corner. "There's only one calzone. What about yours? You couldn't wait. I get it."

"Nah. Not hungry." Owen hadn't been in the mood. Getting dumped did something to a guy's appetite. "You go ahead."

"Owen." Claire gave him a semi-stern, semi-concerned look. "You can't *not* eat Mario's calzones. Here." She offered him a bite from the edge. "I don't want to be the only one who ate garlic."

"About that." Owen cleared his throat. "While we're in costume, you know, maybe that'll be a good time for our pre-rehearsal rehearsal."

Claire bobbled her calzone. "Oh." She caught it and wrapped it back in its crinkly paper. "That's probably true." Her face flamed red. "I mean, you're totally in practice, but it's been a while for me."

It'd been a while for Owen, too, actually. Even though he and Portia were dating, their alone time was small, what with all their other time pressures and being around family and friends all the time.

"I could use the practice, too. Every kiss is different." Kissing Claire would be extremely different. His stomach growled in sudden hunger. "Better give me a bite of that thing."

She held it out for him, and he took a generous bite. The oregano and basil of the sauce combined in a taste-bud explosion. "Mmm. Mario's never disappoints."

Claire took a bite, and apparently, she experienced the same transport into the netherworld of deliciousness, because a moan rose from the back of her throat. "Mmm. I'm so happy right now."

Strangely, Owen felt a glimmer of happiness himself. *What, really?* Well, food and good company could do that, even for a guy who'd been kicked to the curb the night before.

Temporarily kicked.

Meanwhile, it wasn't bad being hand-fed delicious food by a pretty woman on a gorgeous day with a pale blue sky stretching over Lake Sugar.

"My mom was nice to you, I take it?"

"So nice. Beyond nice." Claire took another bite.

Mom hadn't needed an overt hint. She'd just listened to Owen and then acted on her own to go rescue Claire from her over-extended promises with the costumes. When she'd asked why in the world he was auditioning, Owen had mentioned both town tradition and the hope of keeping Portia in town. At the time, Mom had seemed a little less enthusiastic about the play.

Had she had a change of heart about Portia?

Or was it about Claire? His eyes darted her direction. She was happily eating the lunch he'd brought her, humming a Christmas song.

She was soft and supple. Her hair spilled over his arm whenever she reached for another bite, and they rode a while, eating in comfortable silence. Claire was always his comfort. Er, comfortable. Whatever. The spices and her recent touch were getting to him.

They arrived at Claire's house, and he helped her down from the raised truck. "Watch out for the slippery spot on the driveway." If she fell, he'd be doing the play alone. Or with someone else. He had to protect her.

She put the key in the lock. "If you're still hungry, I have some cardamom doughnuts and milk."

With milk? Perfect remedy. He'd probably forget all about his breakup. In fact, with every passing minute, it was becoming a distant memory.

Inside, she took off her coat and scarf, tossing them across her sofa. "It's chilly in here."

"Do you want me to set a fire? I can do that. As long as you don't think Rex Peters is hanging out in your chimney anymore."

"You'd better check." She went to the kitchen and he set the fire. Once a good blaze was rolling, Claire returned with the promised spice-cakes and drinks. "I used wide cups for the milk, in case you like to dunk."

Owen did, in fact, like to dunk a doughnut. A few minutes later, he sank

110

back against the couch, holding his doughnut in one hand and the cold glass of milk in the other. Claire joined him. The fire crackled, its flames better than a sedative.

The couch was older and the springs were a little weak, so they sank toward each other, their shoulders pressing. *I can smell her vanilla candle scent, even over the nutmeg and cardamom and the fire.* Combined, though, they worked through his senses, effectively clearing away other worries and cares. One more breath of the fire's hickory, and the woman beside him was all that existed in the world.

Claire didn't talk, she just let him rest. Finally, he set his empty cup on the coffee table, then took hers and placed it there, too, and then he returned to her side, placing an arm around her, where she fit surprisingly well, and yet, she seemed to be trembling, as if in anticipation.

The kiss was coming. Of course, it was all for the play, but somehow it felt like it wasn't. More like it was something that had been on his backburner for a long, long time, and seemed to be coming to a boil.

He gazed down at Claire. "Maybe we should try on those costumes now." Something made him reach for the silken strands of her hair. They were as smooth as glass.

"We'd have to leave the warmth of the fire." She swallowed visibly. "It's nice here."

It was nice. Very nice. Claire was nice. The way she tilted her head to gaze up at him, with her lower lip caught between her teeth, was nice. Inviting. Enticing. Almost irresistible.

"I don't know much about creating chemistry onstage, but I'm pretty sure I'm feeling some right now." Owen took a swift shallow breath as if he could extinguish the rising fire in him for Claire, but it only fanned their flames. Owen felt something, too—something strong, almost overpowering. "Whatever you're doing, you're doing it just right." He pulled her a little closer, and she complied with no resistance. She loosed her lower lip, glossy and plump. Ready to be kissed. Ready to be ravished. Owen needed that kiss. He needed it more than he needed air.

"You're doing everything right, too." She blinked but kept her eyes on

111

his. It nearly sank his ship.

"Maybe we can do a dry run without trying on the costumes." Owen was her captive, as Claire's green eyes sparkled in the firelight. Her skin glowed, and flecks of gold appeared in her hair. "Don't think about anything else. You're Caroline, and I'm Nicholas, and we've been through so much together. And we're deeply in love."

"I'm Caroline, and you're Nicholas. And I'm in love with you." The intensity of Claire's gaze skyrocketed. "Deeply in love with you."

"So deeply"—Owen tilted his head slightly, moving closer to the kiss— "in love."

A dozen roman candles detonated in Owen at once. This woman, her beauty and goodness, enveloped him. The woman who thought of ways to bring his family together again without Granddad's guiding presence. The woman who would go to any lengths to help a friend and this good town. The woman whose friendship was beginning to mean more and more to him with every passing minute.

Chapter 15

Claire

The fire crackled, and a log fell, sending sparks up the flue, but Claire only caught them in her peripheral vision. All her conscious attention was focused on the feel of Owen's arms around her, on the feathering of his breath against her cheek, on the scent of his cologne.

Portia broke up with him. I can kiss him now and mean it. Because under the weight of his desire-filled gaze, and with the the touch-memory from his hand clasp fresh on her skin, she couldn't separate play-acting from meaning it.

Right now, she didn't have to *dig deep* to conjure up anything feigned for Owen Kingston. It was all present, real, and powerful.

His voice was gravelly, and his breaths were shallow as he inched nearer, pulling her into his embrace.

"Somehow it doesn't feel like a rehearsal."

Owen's face came closer. "No, I agree. It feels more like opening night." He leaned toward her, not waiting for a tilt of her head or for Claire to close the final distance before his arms pulled her tight against him, and he placed his lips against hers.

She closed her eyes, savoring the supple, tender, encompassing touch. His upper lip brushed hers, and the stubble of his shave prickled, causing her to sigh slightly, and to give way to the strength of his kisses.

"Claire," he said, his voice more full of emotion than she'd ever heard it.

"Mmm?" she managed, taking sips of his kisses and savoring them on her soul.

"This is no rehearsal." In a swift motion, Owen placed a kiss so charged with energy that every molecule of Claire's breath disappeared from her lungs.

All her systems went from the slow, steady rhythm of a vintage treadle sewing machine to being run by an electrified machine with double needles and the presser-foot jammed in the full-speed position. If the camera snapped then and the photo went on social media, it might have been flagged for inappropriate content. He leaned her back against the cushions of the sofa, and the heat from the fire couldn't begin to compete with the heat racing through her veins.

When Owen finally relinquished her from captivity, he pulled away. His chest was heaving, as was Claire's. His gaze raked over her face. "What was that?"

"Dang," Claire whispered. "I wasn't expecting ..." *Owen's kiss to feel like that.*

Anyone's kiss to feel like that? Ever?

Owen shook his head. "Me, neither." Owen ran a hand through his short, dark hair. "I don't really want to call *cut* to the scene, but considering what just happened ..." He cleared his throat heavily.

"Um, yeah. Better safe than"—pushing a baby carriage. Because that kiss was leading pretty much one place. Someplace Claire had never been, and had never intended to go without being married.

But Owen's kiss was insanity-inducing.

The perfect blend of Eros and Agape, craving and sincere caring at once. *I care for him. He's my closest guy friend. But that dynamite-like blast of desire!* Whoa.

"I don't know what time it is." Owen ruffled his hair. "Do you need me to take you back to work?"

Much as she should get back, leaving Owen right now felt impossible. She racked her brain for an excuse. "What about our costumes? Still want to try them on?"

"Sure." A smile played at the edge of his mouth. "But in costume, we should probably try that kiss again."

"Maybe at a more G-rated level, though. It's a family audience, remember. Come on." Claire pulled him down the hallway.

"They're in ... your bedroom?" There was a faintly audible gulp in his pause that heated her skin again—the opposite of what she meant to have happen.

"In the sewing room." It had been Claire's teenage bedroom, but she probably shouldn't mention that.

"You have a sewing room at your office and at home?"

"Sure. This used to be my bedroom, back in the day. But I say, if you can have two sewing rooms, you should have two sewing rooms." She pressed the door open with a creaking and flicked on the light. "Behold."

Owen's costume of breeches and a man's Victorian shirt hung from the top of the ajar closet door beside Claire's. Hers was a deep emerald green dress with the tight bodice and full skirt, lace trimming the sleeves, waist, and bottom hem.

"Try it on." She pulled it down and handed it over.

Owen raised a brow. "You're undressing me in your old bedroom?"

"You'll have to try harder for a double-entendre, dude." She pressed the costume against his chest. "A little finesse, please."

"I'll test my costume if you try on yours."

"Deal."

They took different rooms and made the change. Claire paused to examine herself in the mirror. Yes, the hem was just the right measurement. Whew. But there were a few buttons at the back she couldn't quite reach. It was hard to get the full effect.

It was too cliché, though. She couldn't ask him.

His knuckles rapped lightly on the door. "You had a lot of buttons there. Need any—whoa." He peered in through the door, but his jaw was dropped as he gave her the once, then the twice, over. "You look ..."

Claire smoothed the fabric down the sides of her torso. "It's not too ..."

"Nuh-uh. It's not too anything." Owen came toward her. "Miss Caroline,

115

you're a vision." He took her in his arms and pulled her close. "Nicholas finds you absolutely—" His kiss was his adjective.

Still, not family-audience appropriate. He pulled her tight, her back arching, her head tilting. Their height difference was perfect for a truly sensuous kiss. Claire succumbed to it, turning into a supple mass under Owen's expertise.

"Nicholas really loves kissing Caroline."

"Caroline deeply loves Nicholas, too." Er, whoops. "Deeply loves kissing Nicholas, she means."

What was she saying? This was taking double-entendre too far. She dropped her arms and gathered her wits that had fallen on the floor and scattered like a dropped tin of pins. "Let me look at your costume." *I was too busy letting his eyes ravish me to notice the fit earlier.*

"It's great almost everywhere."

"I can see that." The sleeves strained against his upper arms. And against his forearms, actually. The guy had muscles upon muscles. "I'm going to have to let out a few seams here." She patted his arm. "Egad, who needs this many muscles?"

I do. Around me, holding me tight.

Owen was gazing at Claire again.

"What?" Was there a wardrobe malfunction somewhere? Had she failed to complete buttoning a strategic area. "Is something wrong with mine?"

"Nothing. It's just—I'm not going to be able to be Nicholas on stage."

What! Alarm bells sounded, deafening her soul. "Owen, please!"

But he finished his thought. "Not if you're wearing that the whole play." He gathered Claire into his arms, and came in for another attack on her mouth that desperately ached for a constant repeat of his kisses, but the door burst open.

"Hey, gang!" In strode Portia. Claire froze in Owen's arms, and he didn't even twitch a muscle.

"I knew it!" Portia crowded into Claire's room, which had seemed just right for two. Three was definitely a crowd. "Your truck was out front as I expected. I knew you'd be too cold to practice your kiss at the Falls Overlook

116

where everyone else practices their first kisses. I *told* Archie, and he wouldn't listen."

"It's definitely warmer here." Owen dropped his arms, alas. "Hotter, actually."

"I'll just be in the kitchen." Portia backed out. "As you were. Why are your buttons undone, Claire?"

"Uh, just couldn't reach them."

"Of course, of course." Portia waved off her implications. "Anyway, good thinking to get into costume for this. I bet it really helps you conjure up the mood. Getting the right mood is tricky."

No, mood wasn't tricky. Not with Owen. With Owen, mood was easy, like eating soft-serve ice cream, or recognizing letters of the English alphabet. Mood with Owen was Claire's native tongue.

Do not think about native tongues or any other tongues right now.

Claire pulled herself out from beneath Owen's torso, and patted her hair. It was messy on one side, probably from the time on the sofa together. With her fingers, she smoothed it back into submission. *Telltale rats' nest hair!* Mortifying.

Portia poked her head back into the room. "You don't actually need pointers, do you?"

Owen cleared his throat and pulled away, tucking his shirt tail into his breeches. "Don't worry, Portia. We've got it down."

"You have to get it just right. You have to look longingly into one another's eyes. It's all about timing. Too short, and the kiss falls flat. Too long, and the audience gets bored. You're looking for Goldilocks-length. Just right."

Claire met Owen's gaze. A smolder still lingered in his look. Without tracking his eyes back to Portia, he said, low and meaningfully, and causing tingles to explode all over Claire's skin, "I'm sure we can manage."

Owen had been *managing* the kisses incredibly well. His timing was impeccable. None of them had been too short or too long. All had been Goldilocks. Any kiss with Owen would be a Goldilocks kiss.

"Good." Portia clapped once. "Then, you can take me home."

"What?"

"I had Archer drop me off here after we had been, um, running lines together, at the Falls Overlook."

The Falls Overlook! Wasn't that make-out point, more or less? "Archer?" was all she asked though.

"It's a better fit for him than Archie. You know I give people pet names. Anyway, I guess he had some kind of after-school responsibility. He only took off to help me for the afternoon classes, not the extracurricular." She tugged at her earring.

Owen's gaze slid to Claire, who mouthed the words *double-entendre* and bit her lower lip. He lifted his hand to hide his laugh.

"The sides of your eyes are crinkling, Owen Kingston. It's one of your most endearing traits. I'm missing it already." Portia bumped her shoulder against his arm. "Now, take me home. I'm exhausted from all that time battling the wind at the overlook and working on the Evangeline character with Archer."

Claire followed them out into the main room.

"Your costumes are boss." Portia tightened her overcoat belt at her waist. "I'm excited to see mine, too. Sorry I haven't been by the shop to consult yet. Super busy, you know."

"Really? Doing what? Oh, practicing with Archie." Practicing what, though? "I've got the fabric and the measurements. It's my next project."

"Did Owen tell you about my idea for the wings?"

"Wings? Uh, what wings?" Claire took a step back, bumping into the sofa. Wings would be an enormous addition to her workload. "They aren't in the pattern."

"You're Claire Downing, though. You're a sewing pattern engineer."

"Not when I have a deadline." Although, wings would be pretty cool. "I'll see what I can come up with." Portia's belief in her had always driven Claire onward. In fact, Portia was the reason Claire had even started Claire's Originals, despite the fact they'd never seen the light of day.

"Look, I know it's last minute." Portia backed off. "If it's too much, I understand. You've done so much for the play and the town. It's something that can be added to next year's costume maybe. Or I can possibly find some

118

online."

Online wings wouldn't match. Not well enough. If Claire was going to be noted as the costumer in the program, she wanted all of them to be just right.

"Let me see what I can come up with. They can't be heavy. What do you think of molded Styrofoam as a base? We could apply feathers—and spray them with iridescent paint, and—"

"You're a love!" Portia threw her arms around Claire. "The best, the very best." Soon, Claire was hugging back, until Portia said, "Ooh. You smell like Owen's aftershave. What's Owen's aftershave doing in your hair? And why is it such a mess on this side?"

Portia stepped away.

Caught! "Um ..." Claire sipped a quick breath. "You said we should work on our chemistry. We had a few angles to explore." Uh, double-entendre much?

A cloud passed over Portia's face. Was it jealousy? But she was the one who'd dumped Owen. "You are really dedicated to the success of the play."

"Oh, Claire's dedicated, all right," Owen murmured, sending Claire a knowing look. "Very dedicated."

Portia's eyes grew wide. She missed a beat. Then, she burst into laughter. "You two!" She swatted Owen's heavily muscled upper arm. "Now, Owen's got to take me home so I can rest my voice."

"Bye, then." Owen had changed and was heading to the door. "I ... I'll text you, Claire."

He would?

Chapter 16

Owen

Owen rolled through the snowy lane in his truck, humming and tapping the steering wheel. Twice he had to slap himself on the face just to wake back up—because the afternoon with her had been real, not imaginary.

Man, the kisses with Claire had been a revelation. They simultaneously filled and emptied him—leaving him hungry for more. If Portia hadn't come in and interrupted, what Owen might have allowed himself while Claire wore that green dress, he didn't know. It was the perfect shade to set off her hair, to accent her eyes, and to show off her incredible figure. Like an hourglass, but more supple.

They'd been friends forever, but that kiss had been stealthily hiding in the shadows of their relationship—waiting to pounce. *How did I never see her before?*

"How was the kiss with Claire?" Portia interrupted his thoughts. "Nothing special usually happens for a stage kiss, so I really hope you worked hard to prevent that."

"Don't push me, Portia."

"I'm not pushing." She folded her arms over her chest. "Oh, all right. I was. But I saw the way you looked at her. I have to chide you just a little. She's my bestie."

Wince. "How did I look at her?"

"Same as in that photo I took when you guys auditioned. Only … more fizzing live wires on the ground all around you. Crackling, you know?"

Oh, Owen knew. But he'd prefer it if Portia didn't. "Just like between you and Archie. Or, is it Archer these days?"

A sound like a chugging train erupted from Portia. "Chh-chh-what?"

"You and Archie. At the Falls Overlook?"

"Yes, we kissed. Of course we did. He took me to the Falls Overlook. People kiss there—it's basically a rule. But Archie's just helping me so I can get my big break. He knows people."

That's what all the directors said. "You should be careful, Portia."

"Careful? About Archer? He's from so deep in my past that we couldn't carbon date it." She hugged herself tighter and turned toward the window. "You're the one who needs to be careful."

"Who, me?" So that he didn't punch Archie's lights out? "Archie doesn't bother me." The thought made reason stare.

"No, I mean careful with Claire."

"What are you talking about." He didn't phrase it as a question. "Claire is Claire." *Which is saying a whole lot.*

That sewing room in her house hadn't been a bedroom, but the room where he'd changed into his costume obviously used to be where Claire slept as a teenager. Blue ribbons and *best in show* purple ribbons from the Sugarplum County Fair hung on every wall, attached to photos of mind-blowing sewing projects. A few certificates of scholastic achievement were dotted in there, as well as pictures with her sisters and mother, and a few with Claire and Portia. It felt like he'd entered her mind, strolled around, and seen a touch of her past.

A safe place. A place of comfort and peace.

Claire's world.

"She trusts you, Owen."

Of course she did. "I'm a trustworthy guy." *Hello, Owen Kingston here.*

They were almost at her driveway. Portia turned from the window toward him. "I'm saying, I think Rex Peters might actually like her. And he'd be good

121

for her."

"Rex! The stalker?"

"Aw, he's a good fellow with no idea how to approach a beautiful girl like Claire Downing. Lovesick puppy syndrome makes guys do strange things. Trust me, I know. It can even make them agree to direct town Christmas plays."

"What?"

"Never mind." She waved away her slip-up. But it wasn't really necessary. Anyone with eyes could tell Archie lugged a torch the size of the town Christmas tree for Portia. "What I'm saying is, don't get in the way of that. You're Owen Kingston."

"And?"

"And he's Rex Peters."

Her point being? "You're being obtuse."

"Fine, then." She imitated a former president. "Let me be clear." It was pretty funny. Portia could always disarm him. "You are five stars, highly recommend. Any girl in the world is falling all over herself to find a guy like you."

Including Claire? Probably not. She'd never shown any interest. Of course, she was shy. She might not show interest. And he'd been dating her best friend lately. Interest would have been inappropriate. They were friends. Good friends. Friends who now kissed. And would like to kiss again soon, at least on Owen's side.

"Thanks for the compliment. Is the implication that Rex Peters isn't five stars, every girl's dream?"

"Well, he's not not cream of the crop, tip of the top, Owen Kingston, and there we stop. He's ... Rex." Her upper lip curled.

"So are you saying you want him for your best friend?"

"I'm saying that Rex wants her. She's in Sugarplum Falls, and there aren't a ton of single guys who are kind and solid like Rex who aren't spoken for."

"You're saying Rex is a solid guy."

"Originally, I was eyeing somebody else for her, that newly divorced

122

Beau Cabot dude with the two kids, but he's emotionally unavailable since his wife ran off with that rockstar, and so is the widowed bookstore owner, Sam Bartlett. But Rex? He more or less has an *Open for Dating Claire* sign flashing on his chest."

Owen bristled. "He's not right for her."

"Claire isn't getting any younger. She's lonesome and too shy to make a lot of friends. Instead, she needs her own special someone, Owen—someone who will pay her all the attention she secretly craves and who will adore her."

"And that's Rex." Rex was not Claire's equal—intellectually, socially, spiritually, emotionally.

"Rex Peters is charming, in that lost puppy way of his, and Claire does like to take on projects."

Projects. Was that why she'd befriended Owen back in high school? He'd been the failing repeat student athlete, and she'd been the brilliant scholar to tutor him.

His face got hot again.

"Rex could be just that someone for her. Sometimes it's better to find Mr. Right Now than it is to find Mr. Right." Portia jutted her chin almost like a punctuation mark.

"I know you want good things for her, but ..."

"What I'm saying, Owen, is don't let our temporary breakup and your forced kissing sessions with her get in the way of Claire's potential long-term happiness—whether it's with Rex or someone else."

Owen gritted his teeth. Claire with Rex? No. Just no. Worse, being accused of getting in the way of Claire's long-term happiness? If that was the kind of friend Portia thought him to be to Claire ...

"Thanks for taking care of my friend and her fragile feelings." Portia leaned across the chasm between them and placed a cool, dry kiss on his cheek. "You are the most considerate person alive, Owen Kingston." She alighted from the truck and stood facing him. "Which is why I love you. I'll always want what's best for you."

Portia slammed the truck door and shuffle-jogged to her front door and disappeared inside.

Love? She loved him? All these months he'd dated her, waiting to say or hear those words, but to have them come now?

Owen gripped the wheel like his fingers were epoxied to it. He needed to take a drive.

Chapter 17

Claire

It took a full episode of her favorite show for Claire to unbutton the dress, remove it, and press the seams again. She'd have to remember this pattern as a wedding dress, if she ever sewed one. It was perfect in every way. *And Owen hadn't hated it, either.*

Not that wedding dresses and Owen should jump into the same thought patterns.

Except, he was pretty great. And actually available. And those kisses—where on earth had they come from?

No! She had to stop herself before she started believing that play practice was reality. Owen Kingston was her best friend's ex-boyfriend, and one of her best friends. And that was it.

Any wedding bells she might hear chiming in the distant future were for other people.

Not for me.

With a sigh, she hung up the beautiful dress and got to work on designing Portia's wings. Her back room had a few sheets of Styrofoam, packing material from a recent order for the store. She could cut some easily, and then apply strands of white feathers. Maybe she could use that old, white feather boa from Mom's closet and figure out how to deconstruct it, or maybe she could simply wrap it around the lightweight wing-shaped cutouts.

The evening passed as Claire's design began taking shape. No texts came from Owen. He was a guy who did what he said he was going to do.

She checked her phone battery and the settings. Sure enough, the sound was set to silent.

Ooh! A text flashed.

But not from Owen. Was he angry with her? Embarrassed about the kiss? A wave of anxiety passed through her, shaking her kneecaps. *He's regretting the kissing.* Or worse—he'd gotten back together with Portia after realizing that kissing someone else felt wrong.

Bile sloshed in her stomach.

The not-knowing was so much worse.

Geez, blossoming feelings for him put her smack-dab in the center of an emotional mine field. Claire had to slam on the love-brakes immediately. Just because being with him one-on-one was the least lonesome she'd felt in years, and just because he had a great family right here in town, and just because he was a better listener than anyone else in her life—it shouldn't mean they were right for each other. Shah! Come on. Those were necessary but not sufficient for the equation.

No matter what her head and her body chemistry were screaming at her right now.

Case in point, he hadn't texted. The kisses hadn't meant to him what they meant to her.

Another text chimed, and she looked down at the phone. Both the texts were from Rex Peters.

Hey, Claire. It's me, Rex. Got your number from Lulu. Hope that's okay. Before we go ice skating, do you have a date to watch the Waterfall Lights show for Friday night? It's my one night off work for a while. We could see it from the back of my motorcycle.

Hmmm. Rex seemed to assume she'd already said yes about skating.

No, she didn't have a date to the Waterfall Lights. Frankly, she didn't have a date to anything with anyone—and hadn't for a while. What she did have was red-hot make-out sessions with her costar, a man who—an hour ago—took his ex-girlfriend home in his truck and hadn't texted like he'd

126

promised.

Getting asked out for once was flattering. She didn't know Rex well, other than he should brush up on his chimney-diving skills, but wasn't that what a date was for? Getting to know someone to see whether they were a good fit in each other's lives?

Good fit ... She'd certainly fit well beneath Owen Kingston's arm while they were on the sofa watching that mesmerizing fire flicker.

Such a good fit. So had his kiss been—an exquisitely good fit.

But I'm just Claire. I'm not a Sutherland. I'm not a Kingston. I'm not anyone.

Rex was someone, for sure. Everyone knew him, and they liked him. In an *aw, isn't he cute* kind of way. Claire did like cute.

Moreover, Rex was the one who'd texted her.

I'd love to. She hit send, then noted the threat of a motorcycle in the snow, to view the Waterfall Lights show in the subzero temperatures. Of course, he might change his mind and use a different car if she hinted. ***We can take my car.***

In a split second, Rex responded. ***Yes! The tea leaves at The Cider Press were finally correct!***

She could almost picture him doing that end-zone dance.

It's a date!

A date. Claire had a date—after being asked on a date, by someone who clearly admired her and wanted to be with her most.

She let that sink in while she refocused on the wings.

A knock came at the door. Claire scrambled to tighten her bathrobe around herself in case she could be seen through the window curtains.

Please say it's not Rex, anxious to get together soon.

"Just a minute, please." Except, could she in good conscience take the time to get dressed while someone waited outside on the porch in this weather? She dashed to the door. "Mrs. Kingston! What are you doing here?" She invited Owen's mom out of the cold and inside the warm house. "I—I'm sorry about the bathrobe. I was trying on my costume." *And kissing your son.* Her throat tightened. *But not in my bathrobe, I swear! And not without a bathrobe*

127

either. Ugh. With clothes. Fully clothed! Her face burned as if Mrs. Kingston could read her thoughts.

"I'm the one who barged in unannounced." Mrs. Kingston's arms were heaping with flat boxes. "Please, don't mind me. If you'd like to get dressed, I can wait."

Claire made a quick change and returned. By this time, Owen's mother had removed her coat and was warming herself by the fire. The boxes she'd brought were piled on the end of one of the old sofas—where the kissing had happened. Was there glowing supernatural residue as evidence of their kiss—that a man's mother could see with her super-sight?

Yikes.

"Would you like something to drink?"

"Oh, no, dear. I just brought you the finished products so far."

"Already?" It'd only been about seven hours.

"I told you we Kingston Kutters were a force to be reckoned with. We rounded up a few more women from another quilting conclave as well. Everyone did two projects this afternoon, and voilà. What's left? The long skirts for the female roles?"

"Sure. Yeah." The fabric for those was in the sewing room.

"Anything else?"

"The white blouses for the women." The most complex of all the multi-piece projects. "I hate to leave you and your family the most difficult tasks. There are thirteen of them to be done." Unlucky thirteen.

"Believe it or not, a dozen of us are regulars in the club, so if you'd like to come, we could each complete one."

One instead of thirteen sounded like a song of relief. "I'd love that. When?"

"The only time we can all get together is Friday night, right after Owen's meeting he's called us all to attend."

Friday? Claire's date with Rex Peters for the Waterfall Lights was Friday. Ouch. Breaking a date as soon as she'd made one—especially after going on exactly zero dates in ages—didn't feel right. Rex had been so sweet to ask.

Mrs. Kingston readied herself to leave. "You're attending the Kingston family pow-wow, I assume, to talk about the Orchard Lights? It's been a rough year. Having someone fresh there will help."

"Me? I'm just a friend." Claire wouldn't belong. She wasn't a Kingston. And the family might get the wrong idea—that Claire was trying to supplant Portia as the girlfriend. *Am I?*

"Well, Owen thinks the world of you, and I'm about ready to adopt you for all you're doing for him and for us, not to mention for the town. You can't imagine what it's been like—to have my family more or less fall apart." Mrs. Kingston's chin wrinkled, and she swatted at her cheeks.

"Actually …"—Claire looked at her toes—"I might have an idea what that's like."

First, Dad left us all, and then Mom remarried Eddy and left town, and Bailee left the whole country to travel, and Taylor left the family and started her own. Anything nuclear about the Downing family is just gone. Mom and Taylor don't even have the last name Downing anymore.

"Oh, sugar. Come here." Mrs. Kingston pulled her into a hug. "I don't know enough about your family situation to go suggesting you couldn't understand my feelings. It seems like you really do. Would you like to talk about it?"

The hug was encompassing, filling, warmth itself.

"Someday, yes." Very much. It'd be so nice to have a mom-like person to talk to. "But not today."

"That would be wonderful. I can make spice cake doughnuts for us. Owen said they're your favorite." She released Claire from the hug. "For now, I'll just see you at the meeting and the sewing bee, or whatever we're calling it. We'll whip out these blouses in no time!" She pumped a fist in the air.

A grin pulled Claire's mouth. "Perfect."

Well, almost perfect. She still had the date with Rex Peters on Friday.

What to do? The date with a guy who genuinely liked her, versus the magnetic pull of— according to Mrs. Kingston—the guy who "thought the world of her" and whose family who was ready to adopt Claire.

But she'd already told Rex yes. Backing out was rude. And it was his one night off for weeks. What was she supposed to do in this situation?

Chapter 18

Owen

"These look great, Kingston." Archie tromped around the stage, eyeing Owen's creations for the play. "I especially love the angel stand. Portia is going to look ethereal up there." Stars glittered in his eyes. "She's definitely got it."

"It?"

"You know, *it*."

Oh, Owen knew. And he'd thought *it* could be his, up until a few days before. "I'm a lucky man." Plus, she loved him. She'd said so.

Archie halted his tromping. "I—uh. Didn't you two break up?"

"Temporarily. Just until the show ends." He'd been really hurt by how easily she'd seemed to cast him off, but when she'd said she loved him, he'd fallen into a deep hole of confusion.

So confused he hadn't been able to text Claire when he got home.

Claire. Claire was starting to take up a much larger portion of the pie graph of his mental attention.

Even more than his concerns about Dad. Even more than Portia, lately.

Until the *love* word, that was. Now, all Owen could hear was *love* in Portia's voice. Did she? Could she? Or was it a figure of dramatic speech? When she'd climbed out of his truck last night, though, she'd left without so much as a glance back at him.

The woman was whiplash incarnate, and he was a fool for it.

"Temporarily." Archie's brow wrinkled. "I see."

Heat pooled in Owen's gut. "If you don't already know, she broke things off out of compassion for my scruples about the stage kiss with Claire."

"Yeah?" Archie brightened by a single lumen.

"Look, Portia is one of a kind. She's got more than stage-craft *it*. She's also a good human being." She really had cared about Owen's ethics. She cared about the town. She cared about Claire deeply, had actually gone to the effort of pinpointing local guys for Claire to date—while Owen had barely let the thought pass in and out of his mind.

Everyone knew where mere good intentions led. And Owen hadn't followed through on his.

Of course, there was the darker fact that during their breakup, Portia hadn't exactly been pining away for Owen. She'd kissed Archie Holdaway even sooner than Owen had kissed Claire.

What exactly was included in a star's private rehearsal with a director?

Owen's face prickled.

"Good person. Uh-huh." Archie tapped at the screen of his phone. "I'd better get going. Nice work, Owen. Hey, you and Claire. Have you got your stage chemistry squared away yet?"

Flashes of their kissing session at Claire's house, and then the near-kiss interrupted by Portia in Claire's sewing room burst to mind. Those kisses had been a chemical fire—and probably not appropriate for a family audience. "Squared."

"Nice. I could see it from the second you walked into your audition together. I only put Fletch in the leading role out of deference to Portia's request that you be given something small to leave you time to work on the sets."

More evidence of Portia's care for him.

"Which, you've done a marvelous job of, by the way. The crew will love all your innovations for years to come. You're a good sort, Owen. Anyway, better run. It's almost five. I'm meeting Portia for … Never mind. You're not interested in that."

131

Yes, he was. The woman loved him. "Tell her I said hi."

"Don't forget. You're broken up." Archie had no skill at hiding his glee about that fact. But what could Owen do? He'd been kicked to the curb—so that he could freely kiss Claire.

Not all facets of the situation were negative, even if his ethics waged an ongoing, heated debate.

The back door to the theater slammed shut, and Archie was gone, leaving only a pile of questions for Owen to grapple with. When his ethics were on mute, Owen got lost in one overwhelming fact: Claire Downing had a kiss on her. When Owen had kissed her, all other kisses of his past had fallen away. All memories of life before she kissed him had disappeared into thin air. Poof. Nothing existed but Owen and Claire and their kiss.

Portia disappeared, too. Owen grimaced. Temporarily.

Luckily, in the few days since their practice run, the stage kiss in front of others hadn't materialized. Run-throughs hadn't reached the end of the play yet. Good thing. Owen wasn't ready for the fire again yet.

In fact, he wasn't ready for anything with Claire yet. Too many thoughts to sort.

It was Friday, though. He'd have the weekend to work them out.

Owen finished up adding hinges to another set piece.

"Looks good," one of the painters said as she walked through. "My crew are coming in the morning, spending all Saturday on it."

"The list of pieces and their purpose is back there." He aimed a thumb at the shelving. "Call if you need help."

She left, and Owen kept thinking. Obviously, Archie was pushing Owen toward Claire. Less obviously, Portia hadn't been communicating the same messages to Archie about their relationship as she had to Owen.

That, or Archie was only hearing what he wanted to hear.

Or I am.

Archie had it bad for Portia. He clearly wasn't over her, or over whatever relationship they'd shared back in the day. One thing Owen knew, though—Portia wouldn't be leading Archie on. It wasn't in her heart to do something like that.

So, where was Portia's heart? With the love she claimed for Owen, or ... somewhere new?

Owen drummed his fingers against his forearm and frowned.

As soon as the play was over, he would get to the bottom of the Portia and Archie situation, but there was no sense obsessing about it now, when he could do very little about it, by Portia's own edict.

Besides, he had the whole Kingston family puzzle to reassemble, and that, plus the town Christmas play, were projects enough for right now.

Just a second. It was nearly five? The Kingston family meeting that he'd instigated was starting in a few minutes. In a scramble, Owen gathered his scattered power tools and did a cursory sweep of sawdust on the stage, grabbing a few stray screws.

Out in his truck, he made a call. "Mom?" The diesel engine clicked as he prepared to fire it up. "Can you let everyone know I'm on my way?"

"You'd better come soon. Grumbles have begun."

Strange, the Kingstons never used to grumble when they were together. Sure, about politics or sports teams, but not among themselves. "I'll be there shortly."

"Good. I love your idea for us to all go talk with your father while everyone's assembled, too. So don't be any later."

"On my way." He fired up the truck's diesel engine with a clacking roar. "See you in five to ten minutes."

As he went to hang up, Mom caught him. "One moment, son. You didn't fail to invite Claire tonight, did you?"

"Claire?"

"You know, the architect of the reconstruction plan?"

But she wasn't a Kingston. *Except, I did tell her she'd be welcome to join any holiday events with my family.* "I'll try to get in touch with her."

"You can talk to her right this second. I'm handing her the phone."

Wait, what? Mom was with Claire right now? "Mom—?" How—?

"Hello?" Claire's soft tones washed over Owen, sending a smattering of tingles, echoes of her kiss. Everything in the air and inside him turned a peachy pink. "This is Claire." The voice was almost as familiar as his own.

"Hey, what are you doing at my parents' house?"

"We were sewing costumes, but I—I'm just leaving."

No—no, he hadn't meant it that way. "Don't go."

"But I have to."

"Please?" Geez, why was he insisting that she stay? Because Mom wanted him to? *Or because I want to see her?* "It would help me a lot if you could be at our family meeting tonight. I'd like to have you at my side for that. Even better if you'd be the one to explain it." It'd be more palatable coming from someone besides Owen.

"Oh, but I don't think I can."

"Sure, you can. They'll love you." And they'd be less critical of the idea if it hadn't originated with Owen. "Please? Don't go anywhere, at least until I get there."

"Owen—" she said, but he hung up so he could drive.

Owen sped up the tree-lined road toward the white clapboard farmhouse where he grew up, where his whole extended family loitered, likely in hopes of ripping him to shreds, like so much wrapping paper by Christmas afternoon.

"Whoa, dude." Andrew, Owen's cousin the lawyer, put up both hands as if in surrender, when Owen jumped out of his truck, the gravel still spitting from his back tires. "Watch how you park, buddy. You're liable to ram into one of the trees and cut your income."

He could have said *again* without any argument from Owen. Yeah, it'd been a bad crop. But was that all Owen's fault? "Hey, Andrew. Is everyone inside?" He jogged toward the door. If he hurried, he might stop Claire from leaving.

Andrew quickened his step. "Yep, even your sister Odessa, who is, as they say, *great with child.* I was sent out to scout for you. You'd better hurry, though. The natives are getting restless."

Owen tapped the snow out of the treads of his boots as he ascended the porch of the Kingston farm homestead. A huge evergreen wreath decorated the door. It was the house where Dad had grown up and where he now convalesced in the converted library on the main floor.

Dad's whole life had been spent in this white clapboard farmhouse. Even this shadow of a life. The machines keeping his breathing steady clicked in a life-giving rhythm as Owen hustled past.

I'll talk to you later, Dad.

He headed for the kitchen, where he bumped hard into Claire.

"Oh, hey." He got that peachy-pink air inside him again. He hadn't been this close to her offstage for a while. "Wait. Where are you going?" Her coat was over her arm.

"I mentioned I can't stay."

With a quick glance toward the crowded room full of disaffected Kingstons, he took her arms. "Sure, you can." If she was feeling uncomfortable about being at someone else's private family meeting, she shouldn't. "Everyone will love you."

Claire looked stunning tonight. There was something different about her. She was glowing, all put together. But it was more than that. It was that she looked *right* standing in his family's kitchen.

It felt as right to have her here as it did for him to be in the Downing house's kitchen. Comfortable. Comforting.

Until she dropped a bomb on him.

"Um, I have plans." She bit her lips together, looking down at her skirt and heels. "I'm going on a date."

"A date?" The word dropped with a thud. All chatter from the packed front room muffled, and Owen heard only the rushing of his own blood in his ears. "Yeah?" It wasn't any of Owen's business whom Claire dated. It was rude to ask with whom. "With whom?"

She wince-smiled and looked at the door.

Owen smacked his forehead. "Not ... Rex Peters."

"Unlike any other guys in Sugarplum Falls, he *asked* me on a date."

The words hit their mark. Owen truly hadn't ever asked her out. He'd merely attack-kissed her on her couch. Some gentleman.

"He's interested in me. He texted me."

"He stalked you!" Owen's head spun, and he shoved his own lack of texting and bad manners aside. "He dived down the chimney of your childhood home. He's unbalanced, Claire. You're not being serious."

"We've got plans for dinner and then watching the Waterfall Lights."

Only the most romantic of all dates possible this time of year in Sugarplum Falls. Every hackle on Owen's neck rose, while his thoughts scudded here and there for an argument. "The guy ... drives a motorcycle. It's below zero out there. You can't watch the Waterfall Lights on a motorcycle in this weather."

"Yeah, I couldn't agree more." Claire picked at a string on her sweater. "In fact, I offered to drive my car."

She was helping this ill-conceived relationship to bud? Owen's esophagus shrank to the size of one of those coffee straws.

"It's funny"—she half-laughed—"he texted this afternoon and said he wanted to be the one to drive on our date, to prove to me he was taking care of me, so he borrowed his friend's van. It's apparently outfitted with very comfortable seats that fold down flat. We should be able to watch the light show in total comfort."

Fold down flat? A bed! Rex Peters and Claire? Talk about horror show double-entendres. Actually, that was more like a single entendre. Either someone had broken out every single color of Christmas light on the Kingston family tree except the red ones, or else Owen was getting one of those classic anger reactions.

"You can't put yourself into a situation like that. He's taking you to a dark place with a bed, Claire. Does this not raise any flags?"

"Yoo-hoo, Owen?" Mom came into the kitchen. "We can all hear this conversation, just so you know." She gave a sweet, warning smile. "Claire, everyone agreed to Owen's idea that after the meeting we'll go into the library and all sing a couple of carols to his father. Would you like to join us?"

She didn't respond but shot Owen a look like he'd better say something to his mom.

It took a second of blinking for Owen's responses to clear. He turned back to Claire. He couldn't be angry with her. Not with Claire; it wasn't possible. She was too kind, too giving, too concerned about everyone's feelings. She needed friends, people, connections. Who was Owen to prevent that? "Sorry. It's just that I wish you'd stay with me instead. Meet my dad.

136

Sing with my family. Help me tell them about your vision for the Orchard Walk." He took both her hands in his. "I need you."

The final sentence clapped like thunder, echoing as it spread throughout the miles of his internal landscape.

I need you. I need you. I need you. For this meeting, but also ... as a friend. As a consultant and an adviser. *And more? As in, someone he could date?*

Dating Claire wasn't off-limits. He was single. Portia had more or less pushed Claire at him, while at the same time throwing herself at Archie. There was no barrier to this, moral or social. "Cancel your other date. Go out with me instead. You'd like to, right?"

For once, Owen entertained a flicker of doubt over whether a woman would unequivocally want to date him. Sure, that probably meant his ego was outsized, but he knew his worth.

However, when it came to Claire Downing ... *am I good enough?*

Claire ran her own business—all on her own without family support. She was educated, even-keeled, capable, not to mention a beautiful woman who intimidated every guy in Sugarplum Falls enough that they kept their distance—other than Rex Peters who was probably not self-aware enough to realize that she way out-distanced him in every aspect.

Rex Peters, who Claire had agreed to go on a date with tonight.

I want to be a better version of myself when I'm with her. She raises my standards for myself. "Say yes to me, Claire."

137

Chapter 19

Claire

A date? With Owen? All her systems lurched to a halt. It was wrong and right at the same time.

"Canceling now wouldn't be right." This was Rex's only night off for a while. She couldn't simply reschedule. "I'd feel like such a jerk."

"After we finish up with the family meeting, I'll take you out for burgers and shakes at the drive-up."

Claire did love burgers and shakes, even in this weather. And the thought of Owen's company, easy and fraught with potential continuation of kisses, didn't sound too bad either. "But Rex borrowed the van." He'd really given Claire's comfort serious thought, even though—Owen was right. It was a van that practically contained a mattress! The seats could fold all the way down.

"Call him and tell him you're dating me instead."

Was that a slip? By saying dating and not on a date, did he just alter the world? "You mean, going on a date."

"I mean, if you would like to be dating me." He stepped closer. "You would, right?"

Ugh. Of course, she would. "Aren't people, your whole family, waiting in the other room?" Claire should go. Now. Before she compromised her integrity by dumping one guy to go out with another. "I'm hearing discordant tones."

138

"Not until we get this settled." Owen closed the distance between them, placing one hand on the wall behind her, almost pinning her in. "I don't want you going out with other guys, Claire."

Gasp! He didn't? Her mouth dried up like an old fruitcake. She opened it to speak, but nothing came out.

Fortunately, her phone rang. She clumsily patted her coat pocket and tugged it out. *Rex. Shoot.* He was probably wondering where she was! Their scheduled date time had come and gone ten minutes ago.

"Hello? Rex? I'm running late." Her words spilled forth. "I can be at my house in ten minutes to meet you, or you could pick me up at the Kingstons' house. I came to the orchard farmhouse to get some costumes sewed with the Kingston ladies."

"That's just it, Claire." He sounded woozy, like his mouth was filled with cotton. "I'm in the emergency room."

Emergency room! "What's wrong?"

"Minor—it's minor. The doctor said thirty stitches ought to do it. Boy, head wounds really gush, don't they?"

Oh, my goodness. "How did it happen?" Poor Rex. "Are you going to be all right?"

"I'll explain everything later." He coughed a few times. "It's gonna be fine, but our night of dinner and the Waterfall Lights isn't going to happen. Okay?"

"Of course, it's okay. Gosh, Rex. You just be careful. Can I bring you soup?" Soup solved many things. "I mean, not to the ER, but ..."

"That's all right. You're the sweetest thing. That's why I like you so much, Claire." A rumbling and a clatter, and the call ended.

Claire glanced up, and Owen was looking down at her. "Date canceled?" he asked.

"Don't look smug."

"There's a vast difference between smug and thrilled to be getting my way coincidentally." He pulled Claire toward the living room. "Now, let's go convince my family of what a great idea you had."

When would he notice that the idea hadn't been hers? It was a flash of inspiration from Above, and she'd done nothing more than convey it to Owen—who'd recognized it as good.

I guess I'm going to stay.

Chapter 20

Owen

When Owen finally entered the living room, a mutinous aura floated over the group, almost like a gray-green haze.

However, Claire followed him in, and it dispersed quickly. She replaced it with that peachy glow Owen had been encountering all night.

"Hi, everyone. This is Claire Downing."

"You're dating her. We heard." Aunt Karma clapped quickly. "I want to know everything about how you two finally got together—friends for so long. What changed?"

"Not now, Karma," Uncle Chug insisted. "We'll rake Claire and Owen over the relationship coals later. We've got a family meeting."

Ultimately, the meeting with the Kingston family went surprisingly well—thanks to Claire. As expected, with Claire at Owen's side, the extended family was on their best behavior. No veiled insults about Owen's lack of success as a first-year orchard keeper surfaced.

Owen turned the topic over to Claire. "Explain to everyone your vision for the Orchard Walk expansion?"

Her eyes flew open, scared as a bunny. For a second, she spluttered, but Mom came to her rescue. "I heard you want more lights. And music."

Claire warmed to Mom's words, relaxing visibly. "Lots of lights.

Different areas of the orchard with different color schemes. But it will be a gargantuan job. Every Kingston would need to be on deck. Owen said your Granddad in Heaven would be so pleased."

Owen described it more: every tree along a maze-like, mile-long path through the orchard being lit with successive colors of lights, and with music playing as the viewers walked along, and the family paid rapt attention. They even seemed to soften toward him.

"Can the cherry section have pink lights?" Aunt Karma asked. "Cherries blossoms are pink. The lights can be like blossoms. I'll head up that section of the path."

"I want to do white in the apple area." Uncle Chug loved apples the most of all the relatives. "Give me that area. I'll make sure every branch and twig is wrapped with white lights. Does anyone want to help in my section?"

Multiple hands went up. Others offered to help Aunt Karma, while the apricot, plum, peach, and nectarine groves got their own team leaders and volunteer corps.

Tension that had earlier rippled over the surface of the crowd dissipated like steam in the wind.

"You're right, Claire. Granddad would have loved this," Mom said. "Not just the pretty lights, but the way the orchard will be open to the community."

More than that, Granddad would have loved seeing the family come back together. Owen paused, tuning out the hum of discussion, and just listened to the other feeling in the room—the one where he could almost hear Granddad saying, *Good choice, Owen, my boy.*

By choice, did that mean the Orchard lights, or Claire?

Owen owed her. He took her hand, leaning close to her ear to be heard—and to inhale her vanilla scent. "Thank you."

She turned to face him, but he didn't pull away, her mouth was a fraction of an inch from his, and he pressed his lips softly to hers.

Claire sprang back. "Owen!" She touched her neck. "This isn't play practice."

It wasn't practice at all. Truly. This was real life, and with that kiss, he meant to communicate the true depth of feeling growing inside him. "I know it's not. I appreciate you, Claire. So much."

She dropped her jaw as if to say something in response, but Uncle Chug clapped loudly for attention. "What do you say we go sing a few Christmas carols to my oldest brother, give him a merry Christmas, Kingston-style?"

"By singing off-key and forgetting a lot of words?" Odessa chortled and then waddled her pregnant self toward Dad's sickroom. "I'll lead that charge."

The rest of the family herded themselves toward Dad's bedside, where he had been sleeping in the farmhouse library since discharge for home-recovery last January.

Owen hung back, holding Claire's hand. Seeing Dad hurt, even now, after all these months. Owen's error had caused the accident that'd put Dad in his current state. Yes, coming to see him daily had dulled it somewhat, but during the holidays, the edge re-sharpened itself, cutting more deeply than it had for some time.

"Are you okay?" Claire whispered.

No. "Yeah."

"Really?"

"I mean, it's tough, right?"

Wistful and firm, she answered, "It's tough when dads are absent."

Ah, true. Her dad had left their family early in Claire's childhood. "I had my dad a lot longer than you did. He's one of the greats." And he would have really liked Claire. Make that, he would have liked Owen with Claire.

Claire squeezed his hand, which … yeah. It was trembling. "We can stay out here, if you want."

Strains of "Silent Night" filled the air. Even the Kingstons couldn't ruin that song.

Silent night, holy night. All is calm.

Yeah, it had definitely become calmer in the house since the meeting ended and Claire's plan was accepted by the family.

All is bright.

Unity made for a brighter future, for sure.

The lyrics continued until *Sleep in heavenly peace,* which made Owen grab his gut to keep from doubling over in pain. Dad had been sleeping for nearly a year. But was it in peace? Sometimes while Owen sat at Dad's bedside in the evenings so Mom could have a break, Dad's brow clouded and his eyes crunched up. Any responsiveness was heartening, of course, but signs of emotional struggle were hard to watch, especially since there was nothing Owen could do to help.

Owen raced down all these trails mentally, while also retracing the deeply rutted pathways of guilt in his own past. *I put Dad there.* Well, he could have prevented Dad from being here.

"I've never talked about that day." Not with Mom, not with Odessa, not with anyone.

Claire pressed her other hand over the back of his hand that held hers. The security of having his hand fully clasped oiled his jaw.

"Mentally, I know it was a pure accident. Any other tree in the orchard, nicking it with the top of the tractor's cab wouldn't have caused the limb to fall. All our trees are healthy—or so I thought."

"And you were driving the tractor."

The muscles in his neck tightened. "We were getting ready to shake the cherry tree. Dad was inspecting for the best place to latch the shaker's claw to the tree trunk. He motioned for me to inch forward. When I did, a large limb— one that had apparently been weakened by a lightning strike in that big August storm last year—got knocked loose, and its full weight slammed downward. After hitting Dad directly on the head, it pinned him by the neck. I called an ambulance, and for a few minutes, adrenaline gave me strength to pull the whole branch off him and to check his vitals before attempting CPR."

A shuddering breath.

"I couldn't move him to take him to the house. I couldn't tell what was broken. Maybe his spine. Maybe his skull." Owen shook his head. "I couldn't do anything. He was a big, burly man, and I couldn't imagine anything big enough to stop him."

Except Mother Nature.

"He spent months in the hospital, until Mom insisted on bringing him home. She cares for him day and night. All he does is sleep." The feeding tube, the other medical equipment, the ongoing needs—Mom cared for them all.

Owen's inability to prevent the accident had taken not only Dad's life but Mom's, too. "I put on a good show every day, but it's eating me alive."

Gnawing like the tree disease that set in at the wound from the lightning and which further weakened the tree branch to make it fall on Dad.

"Oh, Owen." Claire took Owen in her arms and held him to her heart, saying nothing. Her comfort flowed into him, and he soaked it up like a dry sponge. Another Christmas hymn began in the next room, the lyrics of "O Holy Night" floating in the air around them, but Claire didn't release Owen, and he didn't pull away. "The First Noël" followed, and "Hark, The Herald Angels" ended, too, before Owen had finally received enough of Claire's strength to pull out of her arms and gaze into her shining eyes.

"Thank you." *I needed that.* "I think I'm ready to sing. Want to go with?"

"I'm not the greatest at staying on key."

"You'll fit right in." Taking both her hands in his, he led her across the room to where the library door opened into the hallway. Cousins and aunts and uncles spilled out of the crowded room, but all sang together. "Joy to the World"—Dad's favorite.

"And heaven and nature sing, and heaven and nature sing ..." Owen chimed in at the chorus, his ears attuned to Claire's voice. It wasn't nearly as bad as she'd warned. She wouldn't win one of those TV singing contests, but she wouldn't get kicked out of the church choir, either. "No more will sin and sorrow grow, nor thorns infest the ground ..."

The doorbell rang, and a kid nearly collided with their legs on his way to answer. Who else could be coming to this meeting/party that hadn't arrived yet? Owen numbered his Kingston cousins and relatives. No, everyone had been in the living room.

"Uncle Owen?" The doorbell-dasher tugged on his shirt's hem. It was his nephew, Ellis. "There's someone at the door. I think he forgot that it's Christmastime and not Halloween anymore."

Owen crouched down to listen better. He must have misheard. "What do you mean?"

Ellis shrugged. "He's got a mummy wrap bandage thingie around his head. Hey, that's Claire, right? The pretty girl who you want to kiss all day."

Exactly, but was it written plainly enough on Owen's face that a kid could read it? "This is Claire, yes."

Next, Claire crouched down, too, and took Ellis by the hand, shaking it as if he was twenty-five and not five. "Hey, Ellis. Are you ready for Christmas?"

"Yep! And the mummy at the front door said he's here to take you on a date."

Chapter 21

Claire

The mummy at the front door? It took a few seconds to congeal into sense, but then Rex Peters appeared in the doorway between the hall and the kitchen, his head wrapped in yards of gauze.

"I made it! If we leave right now, we can catch a full sequence of the Waterfall Lights." He reached for Claire's hand. She'd already dropped Owen's clasping grip the second Rex stepped into sight. "I didn't let you down."

"No, you didn't." Not exactly. "But should you be driving? Was it a head wound?"

"Cut only. Not a concussion. Let's go." He pulled her away from Owen.

"Hey." Owen caught Claire's wrist and somewhat yanked her back to his side. "What do you think you're doing?"

"Owen—" In all Claire's life, she'd never once been the object of competitive conversation between two men. It wasn't all it was cracked up to be. Her breathing tightened. "Rex came all this way."

"But he *broke* his date with you, and now you're on a date with me. Burgers and shakes, remember?"

"With you?" Rex's brow darkened. "You've got Portia Sutherland all tied up with a bow. Why would you demand Claire Downing, too? Greedy much? Come on, Claire."

With her gaze darting between the two men, Claire had to make a decision. Both men were correct in their views of the situation: Rex had prior claim on the evening, but Owen had called dibs on Claire when the original plans changed.

"It's my only night off, Claire."

She closed her eyes. Rex had done nothing to deserve her rejection. He'd been nothing but kind and loyal to her. Was it his fault that she and Owen had just shared one of the most tender moments of Claire's life—where Owen had bared his soul to her about the accident he'd witnessed that stole his father's future? Not at all, nor was there any way Rex could have predicted the surging feelings of trust and attraction Claire could no longer deny were brewing inside her for her friend Owen Kingston.

Rex was the epitome of innocent bystander. She couldn't hurt him.

She turned to Owen. "I'm afraid Rex is right. I did promise."

Owen's eyes widened, as if to ask *You'd choose him over me? After what we just felt together?* It was a mixture of disbelief and hurt.

Never in all her days had she wished for two men to vie for her attention. No matter what Claire chose in this moment, someone got hurt.

"Rex, after you called, I told Owen I'd spend the evening with him," she explained. "I wasn't expecting you to come tonight."

The situation only worsened when a commotion broke out in the study. A shout went up, possibly in Owen's uncle Chug's voice—"He's stirring!"

Stirring? Claire's head whipped toward Owen. "Your dad?" She gulped. "You'd better get in there."

Chug's voice commanded the crowd. "Everyone out except Gina and Owen and Odessa. Immediate family only. Out. Out!"

Owen went white as snow. "I have to go."

"You have to," Claire urged. "It's a miracle unfolding."

Owen squeezed her hand, his countenance a perfect mixture of stoicism and excitement.

Hope.

He turned to head into the library. Should Claire wait outside the door, watching for the news, be there to hear the stories when Owen emerged? She sent a silent prayer heavenward that Mr. Kingston would really awaken, and that he would be all right.

"Good luck," she whispered after his disappearance, still torn, wanting to be at his side.

Odessa, Owen's younger sister, nudged through the crowd, one hand on the baby in her pregnant belly, another on her flushed cheek. With red-rimmed glossy eyes, she said, "We've waited so long for some sign. Months!" She disappeared into the library after Owen.

"I can't believe it!" one little kid said. "Uncle Wynn opened his eyes for a second."

The other little kid beside him said, "I bet it's because we sang his favorite song. It woke him up. 'Joy to the World' is going to be my favorite song forever now."

Seriously? Oh, Claire longed to be at Owen's side, helping him process whatever miracle was or wasn't taking place. And yet—she wasn't his wife. She wasn't even his girlfriend. He'd asked her on one date ever, and she was in the process of ditching him partway through it.

The crowd pushed into the hallway, clogging it and shoving Claire into Rex's arms.

Rex clutched her tightly. "I knew you'd do the right thing and keep your promise." Rex pulled her toward the door. "We're not needed here."

True, maybe. Except that Owen had needed her almost like oxygen, or so it had seemed, a few minutes before.

"Claire. We're going to miss the Waterfall Lights if we don't leave right away."

Chapter 22

Owen

Owen rushed into the library. As always, Dad was laid out in his medical bed, the sheet up to his chest. But—it was true. His eyes seemed to be moving.

Mom knelt at Dad's side, clutching his hand, massaging it. "Wynn? Wynn?"

Owen hunched at the opposite side of the bed, and Odessa lumbered in.

"Dad?" she breathed. "Are you really waking up?" She turned to Owen, her eyes wide, her lower lip caught between her teeth. "I need to sit down."

Owen fetched a chair and helped Odessa into it.

"Is this a dream?" she asked, pressing Dad's free hand.

Maybe, maybe not. "I hope not." Too many details felt like wakefulness—including the lingering scent of vanilla on his collar from Claire's hug.

"It started when the family sang the third verse of 'Joy to the World,'" Mom said, not taking her eyes off him. "You know, amazing things happen when Kingstons unite."

Indeed. Especially if it really did continue.

And then—sure enough—Dad's eyes opened!

"Wynn!" Mom cried.

"Dad," said Owen and Odessa. "Hey."

Dad squinted briefly, blinked a few times. No one watching breathed. Was this real? Could it be happening.

"Wynn, you're awake." Mom spoke carefully.

He nodded and rubbed the side of his face. "I need a shave."

Expelled breath popped through the air. It was exactly the kind of thing Dad would say first thing in the morning. Owen clutched the railing on the bed to keep from swirling into the vortex of emotion.

"Gina." Dad smiled up at Mom and spoke in a gravelly tone, likely due to his voice having gone unused for the better part of eleven months. "Wow. How long have I been asleep?"

Odessa clung to Owen's arm, her breath shallow, and not just because of her impending childbirth. "It's really happening, Owen. Finally."

"Owen?" Dad stiffened. "What are you doing here?"

"Dad, I'm right here." Owen came closer. "I'm—I'm so sorry."

Mom tugged Owen backward, whispering. "There's no need to go into that now."

But if Owen didn't, he wouldn't be making good on his bargain—that if Dad could just awaken, Owen would beg for forgiveness.

"Dad—it was my fault. I should have seen how weak the branch was."

"Owen!" Mom hissed. "It's not important."

"Son?" Dad winced, nearly lifting himself to a seated position. Everyone gasped, shocked by the effort. "Like your mother says, we'll discuss that later."

Shot down! Owen couldn't even apologize right, when it came to Dad. "Please, at least let me explain."

But Odessa and Mom stood shoulder to shoulder, pushing Owen back and away from Dad's bedside.

"Wynn, you've had a long year." Mom began the arduous process of explaining to Dad the situation. Little by little, all the time-passage, the events of the year, and the details of Dad's hospitalization and convalescence came out. "Owen has done his best to fill in for you."

Dad frowned and shook his head. "But if the crop was bad—"

If the crop was bad, then Owen was bad. That was what hung in the air.

As if any of this had been Owen's choosing! Further proof that no good deed goes unpunished. The weekends he'd spent even while running his business out of town, coming back to Sugarplum Falls to help Dad in the orchard, as a caretaker in training and as an effort to be a good son, all came to this: naught.

"Wynn—it's been extraordinarily hard on Owen."

"He's not the one laid up in a hospital bed for a year. He's probably still out gallivanting, getting his kicks in life." Dad's neck stretched upward, and his gaze met Owen's over Mom's shoulder. "I'm right, aren't I? You're not spending every waking moment improving the orchard like you should. You don't even care about it, do you? You don't care about this family. You never have."

"Dad—" Odessa touched Dad's shoulder. "Where is this coming from?"

It was true that Dad could be stern, but he'd never been mean like this.

Dad's accusation cut like a thousand knives. "For the past year I've done nothing *but* care about the orchard." But Owen's words came out small, almost inaudible, even to himself.

Mom stepped closer, placing a hand on Owen's arm. "Son, don't listen. It's the TBI talking."

TBI. Traumatic Brain Injury. An acronym the Kingston family had become all too familiar with over the past months of grieving. It could change more than just a person's consciousness; it could cause a total personality shift. A kind, benevolent person could become an angry monster.

"Dad, I'm sorry, okay?" Enough was enough. Owen had prayed and hoped and ached for this moment. Now, all he wanted to do was to get away from it.

Claire—Claire would know how to help him process the experience. Where was she? Owen backed away out of the library and into the hallway. "Claire?" But she was nowhere to be found. "Have you seen Claire?" he asked a straggler, his cousin Andrew, in the kitchen at the cookie buffet.

"Yes, indeed. She's quite the looker. How's your dad, by the way? Did he really wake up?"

"Focus, Andrew. Where's Claire?"

"I think she left with that goofball Rex Peters." Andrew's eyes flew wide.

152

"Don't tell his sister Poppy I called him that, though. Please?"

She wouldn't have just left, not amid the most important moment of Owen's year. She was his friend. She'd wait, right?

Owen scoured the house, the porch, the yard. Her car was still in the driveway, but there was no sign of her. "Claire?" he called into the basement. That's where the sewing machines were. "Are you down here?"

Up through the darkness came a female figure. "Owen, is that you?"

It didn't sound like Claire, but the rushing in his ears could be distorting things.

"I came as soon as I heard." Portia emerged from the darkness of the stairway. "It's the most amazing Christmas miracle." She threw her arms around his neck. "Is this the best gift you could have imagined? Your dad healed, and me back in your arms!"

Chapter 23

Claire

Clackety-clackety-clackety. Something about the older model sewing machine in Mrs. Kingtson's basement caused it to rattle as the needle bobbed up and down, creating the seam.

Claire wiped her brow. She'd chosen the machine closest to the fireplace, while the Kingston Kutters sewed at other stations throughout the room.

Conversation should have centered on Owen's father—and what might happen next—but it seemed like no one dared talk about it, in case of jinxing it. If Owen's dad had awakened, wouldn't they all be happy and excited?

"Another set of buttonholes completed." She placed the blouse in the box for the next seamstress to pick up and add the final hem. "This assembly line is working great. Especially since Archie requested a dozen more complex blouses as costumes at the last minute."

"Glad to have something to take our minds off things," Aunt Karma said. "I think we've all got a lot of nervous energy after what happened the other night."

If only someone would describe it to Claire so she'd know, too. But since she'd left with Rex Peters to watch the Waterfall Lights to get out of the family's way during that sacred time—and since Owen's phone had been shut off—she'd been forced out of the loop.

Worse, Owen's mom hadn't come downstairs to work today, so Claire was doing both sets of buttonholes—on the sleeves and down the fronts of the blouses—to make up for the missing person, and stuck wondering what had happened after she left the farmhouse last.

Why hadn't Owen explained anything? There'd been no rehearsals, and she hadn't seen him at all.

"I'm sure everyone's wondering." Finally, Mrs. Sutherland's words shed some light. "Gina said she'd message us all after she finishes with Wynn at the neurologist," said Odessa's mother-in-law, the high school principal's wife. "I'm just glad Owen had his girlfriend at his side for that awful ordeal."

Ordeal! Claire's foot slipped off the machine's foot pedal. Girlfriend?

But I wasn't there for him. Claire had left. Aching but afraid to ask more, she pulled her messy buttonhole out of the machine and began unstitching the mistakes.

"I guess I shouldn't be surprised at Wynn's temper." Aunt Karma sighed heavily. "Everyone thought of him as the nicest Kingston, but I'm his little sister. I remember how Wynn acted as a bratty kid giving me rug burns and chasing me with snakes, when he *knew* I hated snakes. They say anger is often a side effect of a head injury. Owen did cause the accident, so I can see Wynn taking that and making an issue out of it, especially if he's still healing."

Mr. Kingston had lashed out at Owen? Oh, how awful. Claire ached for him.

More than anything, Owen had wanted to earn his dad's forgiveness for that accident. If his dad had awakened and thrown anger and blame on Owen—for something that Owen already decided was his fault—it must have been an ordeal, more even than these women in Owen's family might've realized.

"If you ask me," Mrs. Sutherland said, "it's when the chips are down that you can tell whether a person will make a good spouse or not. I never thought much of her as a girlfriend for our Owen before, but she had an instinct about last night and was there for him. No question."

She. She who? *Portia?*

"I agree," Aunt Karma chirped. "I wasn't her biggest fan before, no matter how much Gina requested that we give her a chance, but now I'm fully on board the train to Portia." She chuckled at her own joke, and a few of the

155

other women did, too.

Claire's grip slipped, and the seam-ripper's sharp point stabbed her in the fingertip, drawing a perfectly round bead of red blood. The fabric of the white shirt touched it, and it seeped into a red bloom on the bottom buttonhole area. "Oh, shoot!"

All the sewing machines' motors stopped at once, and all eyes were on Claire.

"Sorry." She colored. "I just messed something up. I'll get it fixed." She took the blouse to the bathroom and ran it under cold water, applying some of the white bar soap, and begging the blood to not leave a stain.

How could I have left him?

Her chin trembled as she scrubbed and scrubbed and scrubbed.

Portia had been there for Owen.

And Claire had not.

She set down the shirt before she wore the fabric to threads and picked up her phone to reach out to Owen.

Then again, what could she say? That she'd listened to gossip, that she'd heard he was hurting, that she'd heard he and Portia were back together again? She'd sound like a fool. She leaned her forehead against the wall.

She may not be a good girlfriend for him. But she could be a good friend.

How is your dad? Are you doing all right?

At the very second she hit send, a text popped up. From Owen!

How was your date with Rex?

How could six short words feel so much like a weapon's discharge?

It was no good. She tucked the phone back in her pocket and took the blouse back to the group, which had just completed all the other pieces.

"All done." Aunt Karma beamed as she handed Claire the pile of folded shirts. "Even without Gina's help, we're a powerhouse when it comes to finishing projects, right, ladies? You're a great part of that, too, Claire. Sometimes I wish we could adopt you into the Kingston family. You'd fit right in."

"Don't you mean Portia would fit right in?" she asked under her breath, but luckily no one was listening. "Thank you, everyone. I'll take these and

156

hand them out for the dress rehearsal. The whole town thanks you." She'd make sure Archie put in a big thank-you plug for the Kingston women's sewing contribution to the evening's performance when it went live this weekend.

"You're the one who did the most, Claire." Aunt Karma came and offered her a hug. But it felt hollow, like she should be hugging someone else, not Claire. "We're really looking forward to the performance. We'll be there to cheer on all the stars. I can't believe we know all the main characters in the town Christmas play this year. Isn't it great, ladies? I hear Portia is going to have quite the angel costume."

"Yeah." Claire's voice was flat.

"Very fitting, since she was Owen's angel on his harrowing night." Mrs. Sutherland drew a little halo above her head.

Aunt Karma nodded. "The angel comes in the darkest moments."

And the bad friend abandons. As fast as her legs would move, Claire took her final armload of completed costumes up the stairwell into the main Kingston farmhouse, strode across the floor and out the door into the cold, bright day.

At the shop, Lulu was waiting.

"I'm so excited to watch the town Christmas play."

"Said no one ever." Claire shoved hangers loudly across racks of dresses. "At least we'll have costumes."

"What's with the negativity? You're the star of the show, and I have it on good authority that you've got incredible chemistry with your costar." Her eyebrows went up and down. "What's going on with Owen's dad? I heard some kind of miracle happened."

Lulu certainly heard a lot of things.

"I don't know."

"Really?"

"Don't look so shocked. It's not like I'm Owen's girlfriend." A silent cry closed her throat. "We're just friends."

"If you're friends, all the more reason you should know, don't you think?"

157

Yeah, but at this point, Owen didn't even want to be Claire's friend. He wanted to accuse her of abandoning him, it would seem.

That hadn't been her intent.

Ugh, everything was going wrong.

"Hey, ladies!" The front door bells jingled and in came Portia. "It's costume fitting time!" she trilled. "Which is like Christmas morning and New Year's Eve rolled into one. All the anticipation, the fluttering little elves in my tummy."

"Fluttering elves?" Lulu sniggered. "You have a way with words, Portia. Did you come to see the wings Claire made for your costume? They're amazing."

"Yes!" Portia clapped and jumped up and down. "I can't wait!"

Lulu brought the delicate pieces forth. "She'll have you tie them here and here." She indicated places on Portia's torso. "And they'll wire invisibly at your shoulders so when you move a certain way, they'll appear to flap."

Portia looked at Claire with eyes of love. "You did this? For me?"

Claire tried to pull a smile, but she must have failed.

"What's got you so down in the mouth?" Portia turned to Claire. "You should be on cloud nine with me, since I'm the Christmas angel. Come on, let me lift you right up here with me. I'll show you the view!" She tugged Claire out the front door, from which all of Orchard Street could be seen, all the way down to Lake Sugar.

"Portia, I haven't been in my shop regularly this whole sales season, and—"

"Because you've been bitten by the theater bug."

Claire did feel bitten to the point of being poisoned. "What are you showing me?"

"The *future*." The actress's voice was ominous, as if she were auditioning for the Ghost of Christmas Yet to Come, instead of starring as Evangeline the narrating angel. "Look with me."

Portia extended her arm with a sweeping motion. It would have had more effect if she'd been wearing the white organza bell sleeves of her angel costume, but she still made it work with her puffy parka. "See? That's our

158

past."

"What is?"

"The lake, the Falls Overlook, the dinky little town rec center with its sad excuse for a Christmas tree out front."

"That tree is fifty feet tall and every inch decorated with lights and ornaments." It had taken the town council a full week to transform the evergreen into its current festive splendor. "Don't hate on the tree."

"Fine. It's a pretty good tree." Portia huffed. "But what I'm saying is that a town where Mario's is the one and only Italian restaurant, where there are no more places to shop than a sporting goods store and one boutique—"

"Hey."

"Hey, I love your boutique! I'm just saying it's the only one. Don't misunderstand."

Because Claire's heart was already smarting from everything else, she smirked and said, "I heard you went to see Owen last night."

"I did, but you're changing the subject, and I have something important to tell you."

Important? A rumbling shook her knees like an omen. "Okay?"

"Remember how there were all those weird people watching our rehearsal last week?"

"Weird people?"

"You know, strangers. Not people from Sugarplum Falls. They wore really fashionable clothes and kept whispering."

Claire hadn't noticed. "I was probably too busy trying to remember my lines."

"Whatever. You've known your lines since the first practice." She pushed Claire's shoulder. "You're a natural, I say. You and Owen both. And together, you're dynamite. I don't know why I didn't see it before."

Uh-oh. "See what?"

Portia did another sweep of the arm at the landscape. "Sugarplum Falls, I bid thee farewell. The talent scouts from L.A. have viewed my performance, and they're offering me a shot at the big time."

Now Claire's knees did buckle. She toppled, barely catching herself.

"You're going to L.A.?"

"Before New Year's Day, so I want to leave a-sap. Get my apartment and get settled. It's the opportunity I've been dreaming of! And to think, if it weren't for Archie writing in the part of Evangeline for me, I'd never have had the chance."

Claire's mind was spluttering too much to catch hold on any of the hundred questions competing for dominance. All that came out was a squeaked, "You're leaving? Before the new year?"

"Actually, as soon as the performance is over, I'm outta here."

Outta here. "You mean before Christmas?"

For the first time in the conversation, Portia turned her eyes toward Claire. Her gaze softened. "Oh, Claire. Don't worry. I won't forget you." Her eyes lit up. "Why don't you come with me? I definitely don't want to be stuck alone in a city where I have no friends."

Uh, but that was exactly what would happen to Claire when Portia left. What had been happening to Claire for months and years. "I have my boutique."

Portia's face fell. "Oh, yeah." But she brightened again. "I'll send you daily updates! It's going to be so exciting. The talent scouts told me about some of the productions they're planning for the upcoming theater season, and some of them are plays I've been dying to be in all my life."

She named some plays Claire had heard of and a bunch she hadn't. "It's an incredible opportunity, Porsh." Claire would never begrudge Portia her dream.

"Right? And back to your other question—about Owen."

"Have you told him yet?"

"I wanted you to be the first to know." Portia hugged her. "I just found out an hour ago. It's the most exciting thing of my entire life. Archer was key. I can't imagine what I'd be without him."

Archie. Archie Holdaway. Claire would like to go back in time and keep him from getting hired as the English teacher at Sugarplum Falls High. Then none of this would have happened.

And Portia would still be moping. Portia with a life of excitement was

160

much better than a moping Portia.

"I'm so excited to go!" Portia probably did have fluttering elves in her stomach. "I might not even need a coat this heavy in L.A.." She took off her jacket and threw it in the air.

"How are you going to break the news to Owen?"

"What do you mean *break the news*? Like it's something awful and not something awesome." She huffed, but then she sobered. "You're right. He's kind of a homebody. And plus, he wants me to come and decorate trees or something tomorrow afternoon. I'll tell him then."

"Not now?"

"It's almost the performance, and I don't want to disrupt anything, in case he gets too excited and can't keep his acting face on with all the external excitement. He's good, but he's not a professional yet."

Uh, excitement was one word for it. "I think he deserves to know as soon as possible."

Portia looked at Claire narrowly. "Is there something going on that I don't know about?"

Possibly a lot. Or, then again, if there had been, it was over. "Are you planning on getting back together with Owen?" Claire didn't filter her next statement. "You've been making out with Archie in the meantime."

"With Archie?" An explosion of laughter burst forth. "He's the director! Of course I'm making out with him!"

A sickness sloshed in Claire's stomach. "And would you be doing that in L.A., too?"

A frown crept over Portia's face. "I mean, not necessarily."

Theater people. She huffed a sigh.

"If the lake weren't frozen, I'd throw you in it right now for suggesting what you're obviously suggesting." Portia gave a low growl. "I am not cheating on Owen—not now and not ever. I totally broke up with him. When a couple isn't together, they're not together. So if one of the non-couple kisses someone else, it's *not cheating*. Get that into your head. Why do you think I did it? It's plain as the nose on Rudolph's face. So that I could make out with Archie as his star, which he asked me to do. And so that Owen could kiss you

161

on the stage and not be crushed by guilt. And so that you could kiss my boyfriend and things wouldn't get awkward. But I guess on that level it didn't help. Sorry. I guess I just thought I could arrange it so everyone would win."

None of it felt like winning. It felt like everyone was going to lose. Even Archie. "Give me a break here, Portia. My best friend just told me she's leaving forever."

"Claire, you were my first choice to take with me to L.A."

"I told you, I have the shop."

"You could do the shop in L.A."

Claire didn't want to run a shop in Los Angeles. She didn't want anything to change. "I love Sugarplum Falls, though."

"More than you love me?" Portia put on a faux pout, but only for a second. "I know, I know. You have your life here."

What there was of it. "Won't you be lonely?"

"I mean, sure. But didn't I tell you? I'll be asking the man I love to go with me."

Portia was leaving. And taking Owen.

Claire would be totally alone.

Portia frowned at her. "Why are you turning green? It's not envy-green. Please, don't tell me you're getting sick! Not with the performances happening."

"I'm fine." Lie. Nausea tugged her downward, like she was being pulled over Sugarplum Falls themselves. "Don't worry. I know that skipping the play is not an option!" But when it was over, Claire might as well skip the rest of her life.

At home, she crawled under the blankets, but the sheets never seemed to warm up.

Chapter 24

Owen

Why hadn't Claire texted him back? He'd asked her about her date with Rex, probably in a terse way. Was she upset over that, or was the no-answer-means-leave-me-alone rule in play? After so many months as close friends, it seemed a little harsh of her to shut him out. Especially when he'd been so thrashed at home.

Then, their tech and prop rehearsal had been terrible. Every bit of electricity that had existed on stage between the characters seemed to have been unplugged, dead like old batteries.

Even the kiss was a dud.

"Claire?" he'd tried to ask, but she'd left him standing in the wings.

Something was wrong. Really wrong. But he couldn't get it out of her, and no one else seemed to know.

"Portia? Is something wrong with Claire?"

"Who, Claire? Sure. She was a little sick yesterday. I told her to go home and rest. Seems like it worked, since she made it to rehearsal tonight. She'd better sleep it off tomorrow because if we don't have a Caroline for opening night, I don't know what the town will do. Mutiny?"

Probably not.

Instinct told Owen to head out into the night and check on Claire. Better judgment told him to leave her alone. She was probably off with Rex Peters anyway. That must have been why she hadn't answered Owen's text.

Of course, he hadn't responded to any of hers either. It was too hard to say over a text what was going on with Dad, or with his own feelings. That needed to be done in person, not digitally. And Claire wasn't letting that happen.

What's this pressing need for connection with Claire? Because it's not just our friendship calling to me.

He paced, but slowly. Trudgingly.

Portia noticed. "You feeling okay, Owen? Don't tell me you're sick, too. Claire didn't pass her germs onto you as the two of you were kissing, did she? Because I'll be really annoyed."

Owen frowned. "She'll be okay, right? She has Rex if she needs someone to help her."

"Rex?" Portia lifted a brow. "Don't you read social media? Aren't you following Rex?"

Owen shrugged. "Not anything from Rex Peters."

Archie swept in and stole Portia's attention. "I need to go over some last-minute notes with you on the Evangeline lines."

Poisoned by curiosity, Owen checked social media.

From the look of Rex's dirge poem post, things hadn't worked out between him and Claire.

While that was great, it also left Claire's behavior even more a mystery. Was she smarting over the breakup with Rex?

Why wouldn't she text Owen back?

Have I done something to destroy what we had? Because something had definitely been building between them, and feeling it slip away was the scariest thing since Dad's accident.

Owen had to figure this out. He had to reach Claire.

***

"Is Portia coming today to help us?" Mom asked as she hoisted another strand of pink lights aloft to wrap around the branch of the cherry tree, while Aunt Karma directed the wrapping of another branch. "She came by last night, so we were expecting her today."

164

"I asked her to come." She might or might not. "There's a lot of stuff going on for the performance."

"Yes, Owen. We've been so anxious since we heard the two of you broke up."

"No, we haven't, Karma." Mom's teeth were clenched. "We're letting Owen make his own dating decisions."

Three cheers for his mother. "I'm not sure what my dating status is with Portia." Truly, after last night's display, Owen didn't have the foggiest. *Are we back together then?* he'd asked, only to receive enthusiastic but very vague responses.

Mom shot him a concerned look, but she changed the subject. Again, three cheers for Mom. "We've got quite the turnout for the tree light-stringing. Granddad would have loved this. Go big or go home was always his mantra."

Unfortunately, Dad didn't seem to see the upside of all this work. He complained that the electric bill, plus the cost of buying miles of string lights, was going to drain their savings—what little there was of it after the bad crop year.

"You're thinking about your dad." Mom looked over her shoulder. Aunt Karma had moved to a tree farther down the line. "Give him some time. He doesn't know how much you've done."

"No, he's right. I've been wasting a lot of time." On the wrong things. Possibly on the wrong woman. "Don't worry, in a couple of days the play will be finished. I'll really dive in and do my best for the orchard. I've just got another few hours of commitment and then I'll be able to focus. Which, yeah, I should have been doing."

"Son, it's the off-season." Mom touched his arm. "Even your father didn't work eight-hour days in December, let alone your grandfather. Granddad Kingston knew how to live life."

So had Owen, up to now. He'd been a construction company owner. He'd built it from the ground up. He'd wrenched it to life from nothing. Then, at the drop of a hat, he'd abandoned it to help Dad when Granddad died. And then— yeah. Then everything else happened.

"If I'd been more attentive, the orchard would have done better this year.

Dad's right."

"Do you know what the finances of the orchard were like the first year Granddad took over from his father?"

Of course not. "It doesn't matter. Granddad is legendary."

"You're missing the point, son."

"Look, now that Dad is getting better, I'm not going to be the point person managing the orchard anymore." Assuming Dad healed completely, he'd take over the reins again. "I'm not going to be needed."

What would he do instead? He'd shut down the whole construction business he'd built.

"Your dad will always need you."

"But you agree, he's going to start back on his dream of running this place." Running Kingston Orchards had always been Dad's biggest goal. For a time, Owen's carelessness had stolen that possibility from Dad, but with his restored health, he'd get it again. Owen's wracked-with-guilt days were coming to an end, but Owen also wouldn't have the responsibility he'd taken on for the past year.

Why did that make him feel so empty all of a sudden?

"I agree." Mom frowned. "But he won't be well overnight. He can barely get in and out of a wheelchair at this point. He won't be walking the orchards today or tomorrow."

Sigh. Don't remind him. The healing had only just begun, and Dad had a long road ahead.

"Son, don't let anyone's criticism get to you. You did the best you could as a first-year manager. And it was far better than Granddad's first year. Your father might have been a bear to you last night, but he's been looking over the books today, and he's going to apologize. Trust me."

Yeah, the harsh words still echoed. "I'll take a wait-and-see approach to that. Meanwhile, I'm glad to let him take it back." Sort of. Mostly. Owen glanced around. The trees, in their tidy rows, with their upward-reaching branches, bare and stark against the gray afternoon sky, had taken on a feeling of home for him in the past year. And even more so as he and the family had wrapped each branch lovingly, and retied their family's knots.

Leaving it all to Dad and doing what? *Should* he start his construction business again? What did the future hold in store for Owen, anyway?

For the first time in his adult life, he stood on shifting sands.

"Your dad will be glad to get working again. He loves this place." Mom sighed heavily and changed the subject. "Would you give Claire Downing my thanks for this project? Look how happily everyone is working together. It's amazing. It's the closest we've been emotionally since Granddad's funeral. Why isn't she here to see the lights? I thought for sure she'd like to see this."

Neither woman had come today. "She's not answering my texts."

Mom dropped her strand of lights, and it pooled on her foot. "It's not like Claire to ignore you. She's a real friend."

Friend. Right. Even Mom could tell that their one day of "dating" each other had been a flash in the pan and had ended as soon as it began. Ended with Rex Peters, that was.

"I guess so. You really think I should go check on her?"

Mom's face said, *Yes and do it right now, you dingbat.* "I'll make sure they don't turn on the lights before you get back."

Sigh. "If you insist." But Claire wasn't going to be glad to see him. She was probably blocking his calls because she was too busy dating Rex Peters, now that her heart had been softened by his dirge poem's persuasive power.

Rex Peters! Owen's neck got warm just thinking that guy's name.

"Have fun, son!" Mom shooed him out of the orchard and down the trail toward the parking area, a trail he could walk blind.

At Apple Blossom Boutique an hour later, Claire wasn't there.

"Portia came in, and then Claire took ill all of a sudden." Lulu's fist squeezed and released a few times. Something was bothering her. "I listened, but I'm not really sure what all happened."

"She's sick?" Owen looked around frantically, as if Apple Blossom Boutique held the medicine Claire might need to be healed.

Lulu grimaced. "And during performance week, too."

"That's not important if—" If Claire was ill, who would take care of her? She lived alone. Her family was all in far-flung places. Who would help her, make sure she got medical attention, if something went really wrong? His heart pinched. "Thanks, Lulu."

Owen dashed out to his truck, calling Mom. "Do you have any homemade soup on hand?"

***

"Claire?" Owen leaned on the doorbell. "Are you in here?" Her door was unlocked, as always. Geez, with stalkers about, she should be more careful. "I heard you were sick." He balanced the steaming bowl with its plastic wrap covering so it wouldn't spill and then pressed down on the latch to open the door.

No sound of a television or anything else came from anywhere inside. "Are you here?"

"Go away." A faint answer came from the direction of her bedroom.

Owen peeked his head in. "Hey. I brought you some of my mom's soup."

"Please tell her thank you." The blanket slipped down, and he could see four fingers curled around its hem, plus one of her eyes and some messy hair protrude. "And then, go away." She pulled the blanket back up.

Claire sounded tired but not necessarily sick.

"Tell me what's wrong, at least." Owen pulled a chair away from the desk and sat on it by her bedside. "Claire, please. I'm concerned. Do I need to take you to the doctor?"

"No." The words came muffled through the blankets. "I'll be fine soon. You can tell Portia I won't mess up her show by bailing. Just tell her … whatever you want to tell her."

Owen didn't plan to report anything to Portia. "I came to see you for myself, not for her sake."

As far as he could tell, Portia had caused this situation.

"Thanks for this, but go on now. I'll eat the soup later, just before I come for makeup and cast call." She really did sound like she wanted him to leave. "I appreciate your mom."

But not Owen? He was the one bringing it by. It had been his idea.

Seeing her this way wrenched him. It wasn't Claire. Where was all the light she always radiated? Hidden under a bushel. Er, comforter—covered with little snowflake motifs.

168

"Claire." He resisted the powerful urge to yank aside her hiding-blanket and look her in the eye. "You're sure you're not dying?" What had happened in the shop?

Owen should have responded to her texts the past few days. He shouldn't have abandoned her emotionally after asking her to date him. Her going out with Rex was just more evidence of her good character, not of her rejection of Owen.

Yeah, this moment had Owen Kingston's Fault written all over it.

He honored her request and stood to go. He paused at her doorway. "If I can help in any way—any way—you'll let me know, right? I'm your friend, Claire. That can never change." Ever. No matter what.

I want to be more than her friend. I want to be her protector. The one who spoon-feeds her the soup. The one she pulls the blanket down and confides in when her heart is hurting.

"Thank you, Owen." Her voice was weak. "For all you've been for me."

Past tense! His heart lurched. Everything told him to press for more details, but she turned on her side, and curled up, shutting him out even more.

Out in his truck, he didn't start the engine. He just sat in the freezing cold of the late afternoon and stared at the wintry landscape. From Claire's house, the tip of Lake Sugar's shoreline showed over the treetops. It shimmered in its snow-covered glitter, smooth and slightly pink just before sunset. But the view didn't hold his answer. Nor did the sky.

He pulled out his phone and looked at social media. Rex's post was already loaded with comments, including one from Portia, of all people—sending her condolences.

Blast her. As if Rex had ever been the right person for Claire Downing!

He was not good enough for Claire. No one was. Not even Owen Kingston on his best day.

Habit made him click on Portia's name in the comment section. Her profile was awash in selfies, plus pictures from her past theatrical productions. Where were the pictures with Owen that had been there a few months ago?

Buried, probably, far down the scroll.

He swiped through to see if they even existed, or whether she'd

169

whitewashed him from her news feed when she'd broken up with him.

Some people didn't remove the past. Portia wouldn't—would she? Unless it was to make Owen and his ethics feel more comfortable with the kissing-Claire-onstage situation. As self-centered as Portia could appear at first glance, she really did think others' feelings through most of the time. Well, sometimes.

He scrolled.

Portia in the incredible masterpiece of an angel costume.

Portia putting on stage makeup in the cast dressing room, in front of a large lighted mirror, star-style.

Portia's video of her audition for the town Christmas play, which—wow.

Apparently, it had a title now: *Christmas at Sugarplum Falls.* Appropriate, and kind of obvious. Good for Archie for thinking it up. But whether it would catch on among the real-life people of Sugarplum Falls remained to be seen. Chances were, it would always be known by its generic title.

A notification popped up in red. Portia was typing in her status update bar.

Instead of the expected glowing description of tonight's practice and a plea for all townspeople to come watch her in the show on performance night, Portia announced something else.

Like dropping a bombshell.

Hey, guys! I have some amazing news! An acting agent saw my rehearsal for Christmas at Sugarplum Falls *and made me an offer of representation. Right there on the spot! I'm going to L.A., guys! It's my big break!*

Portia was leaving Sugarplum Falls and traveling hundreds of miles away.

No wonder Claire was sick in bed.

Owen jumped from his truck and charged back inside. Claire was wearing a robe and eating Mom's soup at her kitchen table, the one where they'd endured that bizarre supper club night that had kicked off all this chaos just a few weeks before. The one where Archie had barged into all their plans and changed everything. No question Archie had rounded up the talent scout. No question he was pulling all these strings that were going to pull Claire from her moorings.

"Claire. I just heard about Portia's so-called big break."

"She finally told you?"

"Not personally." Which—that was out of character. Portia normally would be the first to shout it to him. Especially if her words of love had been sincere.

"I saw it on social media. I'm so sorry. I thought if she starred in the play, her roots in Sugarplum Falls would deepen."

"Yeah. I know." Claire's mouth tugged to the side and she set down the spoon beside her soup bowl. "Are you considering moving to L.A. now, too? Because it's not a bad idea for you. If your father is healed by next year's orchard season, the orchard will be his responsibility again, right? And Portia—she's getting a shot at the big time. We all want to support her in that, right?"

When Owen had watched cartoons as a boy, sometimes an animated cat would run into a fan that had a single glove on one of the rotating blades and get slapped over and over.

Now Owen understood how that would feel, and he winced against it.

"Nothing's really keeping you here anymore." Claire tugged at the ends of her hair. "Right?"

"I mean, a few things are."

"Your family will love you no matter where you move."

"Family, sure." But what about Claire? If he'd been confident in her feelings a few days ago, all that fled now under her flat gaze. "That's true. The Kingstons are a loyal bunch."

"You're blessed to have them. I wish you the best, wherever the road may take you, Owen." She set the spoon down and stared into the bowl of broth. "I'll miss our friendship."

The friendship was over? His breathing stopped. She obviously thought he should go. She even wanted him to go. It cut like a knife.

"Me, too," was all he could say before he headed toward the door, leaving her to his mother's soup and her lost friendships that she seemed to have no interest in fostering from a distance.

"See you at the performance."

Yeah. And then maybe never again. Claire was right. Maybe there was nothing left for him here in Sugarplum Falls.

Not if Claire was telling him to go.

Chapter 25

Owen

Owen stood near the power outlet at Kingston Orchard, ready to set up the lights for the evening, when a crunching sound came through the snow. Owen stopped and went toward Dad—who must be taking his first trip outside in a full year. He watched his dad expectantly. Should he really be out in this weather?

"What are you doing here this time of day?" Dad rolled toward Owen in an electric wheelchair. "Don't you have something frivolous to be doing?"

"If you're referring to the town Christmas play, yeah. I do." In fact, Owen should be getting there. Cast call was in a few minutes for the late-afternoon performance. "I was just here to plug in the lights before I go."

It was a gray day—literally and figuratively—and the orchard lights would cast a glow even though it was afternoon. Owen needed all the light he could get. Claire wanted him gone. The orchard didn't need him. He was more or less adrift.

"Your granddad always liked his little light show." Dad harrumphed. "I heard you guys added a few more."

Quite a few. A few thousand more. "Thank Claire."

Claire. The woman who wouldn't leave Owen's mind all last night and all day today as he completed paperwork and payroll and supply orders in the orchard business office, getting things ready to hand back over to Dad when he resumed work at the first of the year.

Without Owen.

"Okay, I will if I see her, but I hear you're the one who orchestrated the whole thing. Well, let's see it." Dad waved his hand in the air. "I hear it's impressive."

Owen flipped the breaker switch that turned on the lights in the first sector—the pink lights for the cherry orchard.

"That's a lot of pink." Dad coughed a couple of times. He'd lost so much weight while he was down. "Is that it?"

"Nah. There's more." Owen switched on the next sector, and the next, and the next. Red, green, white. Blue sparked to life at the end.

Days of concentrated, full-on Kingston-extended-family effort paid off: the whole mountainside was bathed in light.

Dad's mouth fell open. "Son!"

"Pretty good, right?"

For a moment, Dad just gave a series of shallow nods, his mouth still agape. Then he turned to Owen. "You organized this?"

"I mean, everyone helped. Aunt Karma headed up the cherry area." Owen described the other teamwork and leadership that had brought about the Orchard Walk's impressive blaze. "We wanted to honor Granddad. I wanted the family to do something together."

A tear slid down Dad's cheek. "I—I was too hard on you, saying all those things. The crop yield was due to the weather and almost entirely out of your control. After my whole life in the business, I know that better than anyone. Forgive me? You kept the orchard running while I healed. That—that's huge, Owen. I'm in your debt."

"No, Dad. The whole reason you were down was my fault."

"It was an accident. I know that. I was just in pain when I woke up, and it made me say a lot of things I didn't mean."

"If I hadn't—"

"If you hadn't come to help me run the orchard right after Granddad died, it would have fallen into so much more disrepair. I couldn't handle it. My dad's death floored me. You were there to prop me up."

174

"But the tractor. And the branch."

"Did you do it on purpose?"

"No! Dad!"

"See?" Dad folded his arms across his sunken chest. "Enough said. We're letting it go now. Both of us are." He gazed out at the expanse of lights. "Yeah, this display would have made your granddad extremely happy, but the fact that you brought the family back together would have made him even happier."

It was getting late. Owen should hurry to the theater, but how could he, when Dad was here and happy and forgiving Owen? "Thanks, Dad. I didn't want to let you down."

"You never have. Not once. And about the accident, I'm a grown man who should look where he's going!" For the first time, Dad laughed—his big, bellowing chortle. "Served me right."

"Dad."

Dad forged onward. "Now, it's going to be a while, months maybe, before I'm back up to speed. There's nothing I'd love more than to have you by my side to helm this ship of a family business. I hope you weren't planning on going anywhere just because I ... you know, woke up."

Owen had no intention of going anywhere. Not back to the city to renew his construction business. Not away from his family and Sugarplum Falls.

Certainly not with Portia, who would never love anyone as much as she loved the theater.

Most of all, not anywhere out of Claire's influence.

"I'm staying put, Dad."

But I've got lost ground to make up. I need to prove to Claire that I'm not going anywhere, and that I'm worth the risk—and fast.

A seed of an idea planted itself and sprouted quickly, but he was going to need help.

Chapter 26

Claire

Standing in the wings, in the beautiful costume, Claire's stomach was filled with sugarplum fairies—all at war. She gripped the edge of the black curtain, wrinkling it in her fist as her cue approached. She'd crawled out of her pain cave and come to the performance. It was for the town. It mattered to a lot of people, and maybe to Portia the most.

Claire peeked out into the audience, and—there sat Mom and Eddy. They'd come? Oh, and buckle her buttons, there was Taylor—and Bailee. They'd all shown up for her. Why hadn't they said they were coming?

Right. Mom and her surprise visits.

Having family watching should have made her butterflies worse, but it calmed them instead. Friendly faces. People who would love her even if she forgot her lines or tripped and ripped open the bodice on her beautiful costume. Kindness, no matter what.

And check it out—who looked to be enjoying the play the most? Eddy. Wow. He looked so happy beside Mom, and vice versa. Claire should put aside her fears and ask the guy some questions, get to know him, not miss the chance to understand Mom's happiness. Not miss the chance to have a stepdad.

Onstage, Evangeline's narration commanded the audience's full attention from atop the towering stand Owen had built so she could beam down in angelic glory. She had them captive, reacting to every joke, every tense statement. They were eating "Christmas at Sugarplum Falls" right out of her hand.

No doubt, Portia was a prodigious acting talent. Staying here in Sugarplum Falls where she could only perform now and then—and pretty much always the same roles—really must feel stifling.

A little voice whispered in Claire, *It's time to let your friend go.*

The wings on Evangeline's costume rippled under the lights, as if Portia could fly right off the stand and into the rafters and out into the night sky. She did need to fly.

And I need to let her.

Slowly, the wad of black fabric in Claire's hand released, falling back into place. The fairies' battle subsided a pace. Yes, Claire wanted Portia to stay, but there were other people in Sugarplum Falls she could interact with, lots she'd never gotten outside her comfort zone to meet, like the women in the quilting club, or the other cast members of all ages in the Christmas play. Families as tightly knit as the Kingstons had struggles of their own, but they weren't unwilling to admit new people to their circles of connection.

The whole world was full of potential friends.

If Claire hadn't tried something new, thanks to Portia's need to spread her wings—literally—and thanks to Mom's insistence, she might never have realized it.

Of course, she also wouldn't be standing here with a breaking heart, awaiting the impending loss of her two closest friends.

When Owen and Portia left Sugarplum Falls, things would never be the same.

Owen, as Nicholas, entered the stage from the opposite side and his line was her cue.

"I'm here, Nicholas." Claire hurried to him, the lights warming her. Claire slipped into her Caroline role, as if a switch had flipped on.

All nerves washed away. She wasn't Claire. She was Caroline. She recited the lines Archie had penned for her, and shockingly, the audience responded—to her. No, to them. Caroline and Nicholas were as one, and the crowd laughed when they should've and groaned when Nicholas delivered his cheesy joke.

As Nicholas's smile beamed at Caroline, Claire felt every particle of its light, and it lifted her out of the doldrums, out of the fear of loss. If only it had been Owen beaming at Claire that way, but nevertheless—being onstage affected a wild transformation.

I get why Portia craves this. Claire wouldn't want to do it regularly, but it did infuse a wild kind of energy into her. She could do anything as Caroline. She could be funny and brash, warm and engaging.

Confidence.

That was what they called this feeling.

Try something new, Mom said. Well, this is brand new.

When the scene ended, Caroline left the stage at intermission, but she stayed lodged in Claire—deeply. She hustled to a dark corner and sent a text to Lulu quickly before any of this adrenaline wore off.

Could you do me a favor asap and dress one of the front window mannequins with a Claire Original? You know where they are, right?

Lulu shot back with an all-caps YES, but she'd been watching the show.

I'm in the foyer getting refreshments. You're amazing onstage, by the way. You and Owen, good grief. You're bringing down the house with all your chemistry. You should hear the comments out here. They can't believe that's you up there. Of course, I've seen it coming for months. Years, really. He was always hanging around the shop, kind of panting after you. Anyway, do you want me to leave the play and put out the dress now? I'll do it! I can go and be back before the final stage kiss. Something I don't want to miss!

Neither did Claire. A final farewell to Owen. She might not be able to do it without crying.

Luckily, the script called for tears at that point in the story.

They wouldn't be fake.

Chapter 27

Owen

"Oh, Nicholas. I have never seen a sickroom look so festive." Claire's character Caroline had tears glistening in her eyes.

The final kiss of the play loomed between them, coming like a freight train without brakes. Owen hadn't kissed her during run-throughs. She'd always stepped back from him and said aloud, *And then we kiss. Yay. The end.* Archie hadn't insisted on the affection, too busy staring at Portia or consulting with her.

No doubt Archie was going to really miss Portia when she left him for the bright lights of the big city.

Claire delivered Caroline's next line. The kiss was next. Owen swallowed, his Adam's apple making a sound he hoped didn't carry into the cheap seats, and then said, "It's all for you, Caroline. Every inch of it, from the bottom of the trunk to the angel on the top of the Christmas tree."

He took Claire in his arms. Their eyes met, and hers were brimming. They triggered his own tear ducts—which had never happened to him before. "Merry Christmas, Caroline."

They held the gaze a moment longer, Owen's heart speeding up, a heat spreading through him that didn't emanate from the stage lights.

"Merry Christmas, Nicholas," she said, her full lips parting, making that

179

pinkish glow ignite inside him, far more brilliant than all the cherry section at the orchard. The flat of her hands pressed against his chest, and he placed his hands on the dip at her waist.

With a tremble, Owen placed a tender kiss on her lips. Her wet cheek brushed his as he pressed the kiss a second time, more firmly and with greater meaning.

Wait, wet? Was she really crying? The script called for it, but this didn't look like acting.

"I love you, Caroline."

"I love you, too, Owen." She rested her cheek against his chest, and the lights dimmed. The audience broke into applause as the curtains whisked closed, but Claire didn't move from his embrace. His shirt grew damper, and he pulled her closer to him.

The curtains opened again, and the embrace had to make way for the various groups from the play to receive their accolades from the audience. Still, though, Claire clung to him as if this was the end of something bigger than just a run of a Christmas play.

They took their bows, and the audience's cheers were deafening.

"They love you, Claire." *Just like I do.* "You were the star."

"Portia was the star," Claire shouted.

They stepped aside so that Portia could bow and catch the roses being thrown at her from the crowd. Archie probably set that up ahead of time, knowing him. The consummate showman.

"I'm going out in the lobby to visit with people." Claire patted his arm. "Goodbye, Owen. It's been amazing."

"What do you mean, goodbye?"

She slipped down the stairway into the crowd. Owen chased her, but he was stopped by bevy after bevy of Sugarplum Falls citizenry.

"Well, well, well. Now we can see why it's rightly named the Kingston Theater. You owned that stage, Owen, dear."

"Nicholas and Caroline were at their decades-long peak. That kiss at the end. I was weeping!"

"You had the whole place in tears, Owen Kingston. I wouldn't be surprised if you heard Hollywood calling."

"Hollywood. Ha." Owen pulled aside, but they followed him, and more women of all ages swarmed him. Some teenage girls wanted his autograph. It was no use trying to catch up with Claire now. But—he had something important to tell her. To show her.

I need to be with her.

"Hey, guys." Portia appeared at Owen's side. "Owen? Can I steal you away from your adoring fans for a bit?" She turned to the women surrounding him. "Sorry, ladies. He's mine for now."

If there was one thing about Portia Sutherland, it was that people didn't argue with her when she wanted something. Freed from the clutches, Owen gladly exited out the back of the theater with Portia.

"Can you take me for a drive? There's something I want to talk to you about."

"Can't we talk here?" Claire was inside, and Owen couldn't miss her. "Claire's—"

"Yeah, isn't it great that her family all came? She's with them now, I think."

Oh. Owen's shoulders fell. "I'm still in costume, and ..."

"It's almost like you don't want to be with me." Portia clung to his side and pulled him into the cast parking lot. "Worry about that later. This is important."

Soon, they were driving through the streets of Sugarplum Falls. Every house had lights on the eaves, wreaths on front doors, ribbons on the mailbox poles.

Portia heaved a sigh. "It's so idyllic. Sometimes I never want to leave."

"Yeah?" Owen turned down Orchard Street toward the main area of town. "Same. I love it here. Especially now that Dad's on the mend."

"Good for him, right? And since he won't need you ..."

For a second, Portia sounded uncertain, a wholly unfamiliar demeanor for her. Owen stole a glance, and she was biting her thumb.

"What's wrong?"

"Everything will be wrong if you don't go with me to Los Angeles."

181

He swerved but righted the steering. "Me?" A cough closed his throat.

"Of course, you." Portia scooted over beside him on the bench and placed her curled, cool fingers against his neck. "You're Owen Kingston. My boyfriend."

"We broke up, Portia." He pulled over to the side of the road at a place with a view of the falls. Christmas Eve, and the cars were thick, lining up already for the Waterfall Lights show. "You broke up with me, to be more precise."

"Only until the play was over, and now it's over, and life is moving *on.*"

She had that right, at least. "You're leaving Sugarplum Falls, and—"

"And you're coming with. Think of it, Owen. You and me in the city. Different restaurants every night. Well, nights when I'm not working on shows. But we'll experience all the glitz and glamour together."

Huh. Owen had not seen this coming. At all. And he wanted nothing to do with glitz, unless it involved adding twice as many lights to Kingston Orchard next year.

"Out of curiosity, how do you see me fitting into that world?"

"I mean." She looked down at her nails. "You built those amazing sets." She looked up at him, brightening. "You weren't half bad on the stage, either. I bet you could land a role or two. You do have stage presence."

"I'm not interested in acting anymore." On any level. "Portia, I'm afraid—"

"I know that, which is why I said the set-building crew thing first. Please, Owen. I won't have my bearings without you. I need you."

A little place in his heart still held feelings for her. She'd been a perfect placeholder in his heart and for his escape time while he'd taken over the orchard for the past year. "We were good together."

"And we can be again!"

"I had some fun times, honestly."

"You're putting everything in the past tense, Owen."

He was. At least with Portia. "Be honest, Portia. All our very best times weren't just the two of us. They were always also with Claire."

"Sure. Claire is wonderful. She's been my closest friend for years, and—"

182

Portia stopped short. "Oh, my word." She slapped her forehead and let her palm slide down her cheek. "I can't believe I didn't see this coming."

"See what coming?" But of course she meant Owen's newly discovered love for Claire.

"I'm such a fool." Portia slid away from him on the bench. "And to think—I more or less pushed the two of you together. The stage kiss, the time in rehearsals, all of it." Her voice took on an anxious quality. "Owen, please. Don't mistake that for reality. Leading man and leading lady romances erupt all the time in the theater, but they're almost never lasting." She cited a dozen or more couples from Hollywood that sounded vaguely familiar. "See? I'm telling you, you have to forget that. You and Claire were a great stage couple. The chemistry was off the charts. That's why I posted the picture. But it wasn't so that you'd dump me."

"I can't dump you, Portia. I'm the dumpee here." Owen needed to end this conversation. There was no point in prolonging it. "I actually have to thank you for what you did. If we hadn't been cast together in the play, I don't know if I would have ever seen Claire for what she is—the perfect woman for me. My other half. My ideal ... everything."

"Owen, please. Wait."

"I shouldn't wait, though, Portia. I've waited far too long for the wakeup call, and you're the one who sounded it. I'll always be grateful. But now, I have something really important I have to do."

"But what about coming with me to Los Angeles, what about being my rock? What about us? You promised we'd get together after the play ended."

Owen hadn't promised anything of the sort. He reached for Portia's hand and squeezed it for a minute. "You said that a stage production was a mini-cosmos of reality. I had wanted time with you, to see whether we could work out, and you gave me that. Thanks. It's all clear now, and something else is clear—there's a Mr. Right for you. Or at least a Mr. Right Now." Using her corny term on her felt like a low blow. "You and I both know who it is that wants desperately to go experience the big city with you. The man who will go to extreme lengths to make you the star—of everything."

"You mean Archie."

"Don't let his efforts go unnoticed."

"He does have a good stage kiss. Among other good qualities." Portia heaved a sigh. "It's just … he's not Owen Kingston."

"No, but he's Archie Holdaway. And he's crazy-dog in love with you."

"And you're in love with my best friend Claire."

"I am."

Portia looked crestfallen. "You're choosing her."

"I am. But don't worry. Archie—he's going to take you to the places your heart wants to go. My heart is in Sugarplum Falls."

"And I need to see the world." She nodded with resignation. "Claire is a lucky woman."

No, Owen was the lucky one. "And Archie is a lucky man."

"Good-bye, Owen." Portia sipped a breath and let it out heavily.

Owen took Portia back to the theater, where she searched out Archie to give him the offer of his lifetime. The low-bass shout of delight that erupted from the green room downstairs told Owen everything he needed to know about who was going to Los Angeles.

Unfortunately, Claire was nowhere to be found at the theater.

Fingers crossed, she had already gone back to her house—and that Owen's plan for Christmas Eve for Claire was working out according to plan.

He'd been absent from it for far too long already. He climbed in his truck and broke all the speed limits to get to the Downing house. He'd go down the chimney if he had to.

Chapter 28

Claire

The second the crowd dispersed, Claire hustled to change out of her costume.

"We'll meet you at the house for Christmas Eve traditions!" Bailee had said, hugging Claire with her bronze-tanned arms. "I call the first spice doughnut in the morning."

Something told her she should at least say goodbye to Owen for real. It was rude to only say it onstage. And worse, she'd messed up her line—switching his name for Nicholas's. No one had chided her about it, thank goodness.

They'd been friends too long for her to treat him that way. She needed to make things right. But, Owen wasn't near the dressing rooms, and he wasn't anywhere being detained by female fans.

Maybe he'd already left with Portia.

"Have you seen Owen?" Claire stopped George Milliken on the back stairway.

"Left with Portia Sutherland a while ago." Mr. Milliken aimed a thumb at the back door. "Maybe he's just in his truck with her in the parking lot. You want me to check?"

"I can."

"Great job as Caroline, by the way. You were a revelation."

"Thank you." How sweet.

In the alleyway out back, only Declan's bike leaning against the red door was visible in the pale streetlight.

Other cast members streamed out the back door, but no Owen. Claire reached for her phone to dial him, but there was no answer.

Home. That was the answer now. Mom and Eddy and everyone were waiting, but maybe she could arrange to have Owen come by, even though it would rip open a wound in her.

Someone would someday come and stitch her up.

Maybe.

Okay, probably not.

For sure, Rex Peters wasn't the answer, but someone else might move to town. Someday. Maybe Lulu had a nephew. She'd never asked Lulu to set her up on dates. They would pale by comparison to Owen Kingston.

She plodded through the falling snow toward her car and aimed it for home.

The glaring fact remained that Claire was head-over-heels in love with Owen Kingston. And in hindsight, she would have been for a good, long time if there hadn't been hugely obvious reasons not to be. He was everything she'd ever dreamed of in a guy and more. He was strong and responsible. He loved his family to the point of giving up his business and shifting careers at the drop of the hat to help them. He cared about right and wrong. He loved Sugarplum Falls and the people in it, enough that he even stepped miles outside his comfort zone to make sure their town traditions stayed alive.

More personally, he was the world's greatest listener, and the way he kissed Claire made her feel like someone had plugged in all the strands of lights on her internal Christmas tree.

Getting over that would take a long time.

Claire turned onto her street. Wow, there sure were a slew of cars lined up in front of the neighbor's house. One even partially blocked her driveway. Great, someone had actually parked *in* Claire's driveway. Rude.

All the lights were off in her house, but as she climbed onto the porch, voices reached her ears. Someone was inside! And the voices weren't her

186

family's.

Oh, no. Not again! Owen had warned her to lock her doors. Just because this was Sugarplum Falls didn't mean it was a town free of people willing to intrude in her house. The incident with Rex on the rooftop should have taught her that lesson weeks ago.

"She's here!" someone inside hiss-whispered. "Get ready!"

Fear gripped her heart. Claire stepped backward, toppling onto her bottom in the snow. She turned over and scrambled back toward her car. If she got away fast enough, she could get to the police station, and—

"Claire!" The porch light blazed on. "Where are you going?"

Claire froze in her tracks. "Mrs. Kingston?"

"Surprise?" Mrs. Kingston half-laughed. "We really should have told you we were here, at least by letting the lights be on, but your mom is here and insisted a surprise was best. I guess I forgot about your incident with the wannabe Santa coming down the chimney. We didn't mean to scare you."

"But—what are you doing here?" Claire's heart rate returned to a more reasonable beat. "Is Owen inside?"

"No." Mrs. Kingston took her by the arm and led her in. "We heard you liked supper clubs, so we brought supper."

"And flowers!" Ellis, the little Kingston nephew jumped up and down on Claire's old couch. "Look!"

On the coffee table was the biggest cellophane-wrapped bouquet of roses she'd ever seen. "There have to be three dozen!" Claire gasped.

"Long-stemmed." A niece beamed. "Long-stemmed roses mean *love*."

Claire's mouth went dry. What exactly was going on here? It was six o'clock on Christmas Eve. But, looking around, there had to be three dozen people in her house, all holding plates of food and talking one with another or looking at her expectantly.

But Owen wasn't one of them. He'd gone off with Portia, and neither one was here.

Aunt Karma came up to her immediately holding out a plate of holiday food—all the favorites. "Would you like some Granny Smith apple pie after dinner? We made it with apples from our orchard."

187

"Sure." Claire accepted the large, sturdy paper plate filled with stuffing, roast turkey, homemade dinner rolls, berry jam, green beans, and lots more. It weighed about two pounds. "Who made all this?"

"Everyone contributed," Aunt Karma said. "That's how the Kingstons do it. We'd never dream of letting just one person be stuck making the entire meal."

Suddenly, Owen's doggedness about bringing the box of apples to her first, failed supper club made sense. And all the other times he'd brought food or drinks or chips or whatever to the get-togethers they'd had with Portia.

"It sounds like a better way to run a supper club."

"Absolutely," Mrs. Kingston said through a bite of stuffing. Claire tasted hers. Mmm. Sausage and pecans were included in the recipe. "And there's a lot more pie when we're done. Apricot, cherry, peach. Owen said fruit pie is your favorite."

"All pie is my favorite. I think I still have some cans of whipped cream in my fridge."

"Oh, we found them." The niece came up, grinning, a blob of whipped cream on her face. "But we used them up and made more. Whipped cream is the most important part of the meal."

Claire would not argue. She just took another bite from her plate. This green bean recipe had bacon and mushrooms. So delicious.

Now, about fifty people in all milled around. Not just Aunt Karma's and Uncle Chug's family. Mom and Eddy were in conversation with them, too. Bailee and Taylor were in the kitchen with some of the Kingston Kutters.

She didn't know names, but she was recognizing faces, including Owen's dad's. His chair was parked beside Mrs. Kingston.

It suddenly felt like everyone was family, hers and theirs and all were one.

Including Claire.

The miracle of trying something new was unfolding before her eyes.

"In case you're wondering, this is what the Kingstons do." Aunt Karma beamed. "We insinuate ourselves into everyone's lives—and raid their refrigerators."

Portia and Owen were nowhere in sight, however. Just a milling hoard of Kingstons, laughing and making Claire's home their own. Claire took another bite of the holiday meal. Mmm. Whoever made this cranberry sauce used a very good recipe, or else they sprinkled Christmas magic all over it.

"The flowers are for you." Ellis carried one of the long-stemmed roses from the bouquet. "Because you did a good job kissing my uncle on the stage."

Ellis's mother came and swept him up. "Sorry, Claire. He's just happy that Owen found someone wonderful like you. We all are."

They were? And ... he had? What exactly—

Mrs. Kingston came and took Claire by the elbow. "Come say hi to Owen's dad." She led Claire toward a man seated in a wheelchair near the fireplace. "Wynn, you remember Claire Downing."

Trepidation filled Claire. The guy had allegedly chewed out Owen for not taking the orchard seriously, and Portia had flown to Owen's side in the aftermath. But ... was there more to the story?

"Claire Downing!" He had a booming voice, despite his slight frame. The man who'd lain in a hospital bed in Owen's parents' home for the past year looked like someone who used to be burly, and who could be again, given continued nourishment and probably some physical therapy. "I hear you're the one to blame for all of this."

Instead of a cranky-old-man flash in his gaze, his eyes twinkled, and his cheeks rounded.

"Blame! Wynn, don't tease her. She doesn't know you yet."

But the teasing was perfect. It wrapped Claire immediately into the family dynamic. "It's all right, Mrs. Kingston."

"Gina. Call me Gina."

Claire extended a handshake to Owen's dad. "Your son has been a good friend to me. And he thinks the world of you, even though you laughed when he lost his scooter in the snow."

The image of it, now that Claire pictured it, really did seem comical.

Mr. Kingston erupted in laughter again. "See, Gina? She's one of us. She can tease Owen without even being prompted. I like her. Plus, we owe her for reapplying the glue of the family." He turned back to Claire. "Have you seen

189

the lights of the Orchard Walk yet? Oh, what a dumb question. Of course you have. They were your brainchild. You probably supervised."

"Not at all." Had they gone up? "I've been in the play, and ..." And Owen hadn't invited her, or if he had tried, she'd shut him down. A mistake, for sure. "I haven't seen the orchard all lit up. Is it pretty?"

"Pretty!" he boomed. "It's spectacular! It's better than any of those theme parks or those massive national fireworks shows. It's light enough you could probably see it from space."

Mrs. Kingston grin-frowned and leaned in to Claire's ear to whisper, "As long as you weren't too far out into space. Like say, higher than an airplane."

Mr. Kingston tugged at the hem of her festive sweater. "Hey. I'm trying to sell it to her. Don't fact-check my sales pitch."

"Of course not!" Gina wore a wily grin.

The two had a wacky dynamic, but it was fun. Claire hadn't seen a fun family at play as a kid, so this was new. Mrs. Kingston looked overjoyed to have her husband back, beaming and touching his shoulder over and over.

"I'd love to see the orchard lights."

"We'll go now!" Mr. Kingston declared. "Come on. Everyone's planning on it."

With some fanfare, the kitchen was cleaned, the house was tidied, and the whole crowd made a mass exodus to their cars—all in a matter of a few minutes. Chaos seemed to reign, but it was a controlled chaos. The little kids had clearly eaten too much sugar, as they were bouncing on every surface, but the bustle was lively, irresistible.

"I'll meet you there?" Claire stood on the front porch as everyone climbed in their cars, only a little sad to be going without Owen. "You leaving, Mom?"

Mom and Eddy and the girls were heading back tonight. "This was wonderful. The Kingstons are always so kind. You take care, honey. We'll see you for New Year's?" Mom hugged her. "I saw Lulu, by the way. She told me about Claire's Originals going up in the store."

Claire hunched her shoulders. "It's time."

"Yes. It is." Mom gave her one more hug. "Thanks for giving us a merry

Christmas, sweetheart. I'm so proud of you for trying lots of new things. And for just being you."

"I love you." She hugged Mom back. And then grabbed Eddy's hand. "Let's talk sometime."

"I'd like that. You were great in the play, Claire. Merry Christmas." Eddy and Mom left, and Claire headed toward her car to make the drive to the orchard.

Mrs. Kingston had already loaded Mr. Kingston and his wheelchair into her SUV. "You're riding with me, darling."

Darling. Really? Claire didn't resist. They traveled to the orchard. As they grew nearer, the sky gave off a pastel glow.

"Oh, look at it!" As they pulled into the parking lot of the playground where the original light show had been, suddenly, thousands more lights blazed to life. A pink group, a green group, a blue, a red, a white—*bam! bam! bam!*— as if switches were being thrown. And they probably were.

But by whom?

"It's incredible," Claire breathed.

Mrs. Kingston turned around from the driver's seat and smiled. "It's more than just light. It's family, together again."

Warmth tingled from Claire's scalp, down her neck and spine, and through her legs to her toes. "Beautiful."

"Yes, you are." Owen had opened the door of the car and extended his hand to help her out. "Would you like to go on the Orchard Walk with me?"

"Owen!" But ... "You're here."

He'd thrown the light switches, it would seem. "Sure. Of course. And so are you."

"But, where's Portia?"

"Celebrating with Archie."

"Archie!" Claire accepted his hand in her own, and the warm tingles from the lights seemed like they'd been only a one on the tingle-scale. Touching Owen's hand was a ten. She turned back to see what his parents were doing, but Mrs. Kingston waved them on.

"Go on, kids. We'll see you on the hill with everyone else."

191

"The hill?" she asked. "What is going on?"

"You'll see. For now, walk with me."

He could have said *float beside me*. Claire's feet only touched air. Owen was here! He wasn't going to Los Angeles! Except … there was a lot she was missing.

"What exactly happened. Portia said—" She'd said she was going to take the man she loved to Los Angeles with her. And she'd definitely meant Owen. "I thought she wanted you to go with her."

Owen lowered his voice. "She did ask."

Claire walked beside him, but her spirit was sitting on the thorns of anticipation. "But you aren't going."

He turned to her. "How could I, when I'm in love with you?"

All the thorns dissolved, and only wings remained—and Claire flew on them as Owen took her in his arms, looking down into her eyes with something new in his gaze.

He's mine. And I want to be his, too.

"You"—her voice trembled, and she swallowed hard to try to steady it— "you're in love with me?"

"I am, Claire." His stare blazed, warming her. "I have been for longer than I knew."

He loved her. He'd loved her a long time. They were in love! Claire could fly, could soar over the trees, over the orchard, over the mountains and the waterfall and the world.

Owen loves me! Should she tell him how she felt, too? She opened her mouth to confess, but a different phrase spilled out. "I must say, that's a good thing."

"Oh? You mean the fact I'm in love with you?" When Claire nodded, Owen asked with a broad grin, "Why's that?"

"For one thing, because Archie is in love with Portia." That fact had been more than obvious, ever since Archie had come back to Sugarplum Falls. In fact, his choice to direct the play might have simply been a way to try to get Portia back into his life. He would take Portia to the places her heart wanted to go—and chances were, she'd soon realize that he was the right man for her.

192

"And she might be in love with him back, as soon as she realizes how right he is for her."

"And for another?" he asked.

"And for another, because I'm totally in love with you." Saying it aloud created an electricity in her, a confirming bolt of truth that shot from her head to her toes. "I love you, Owen Kingston."

She hugged him close and rested her head against his chest. His heartbeat thudded softly in her ear, *I love you, I love you, I love you.*

Owen rubbed her back. "Every happy moment I've had in the past year involved you, Claire. From the picnics in the spring to the movie nights in the summer, to the craziness of the town Christmas play this fall."

"We weren't dating, though." He'd been dating Portia. Who could look at Claire when Portia was around?

"No, but it wasn't more than a few weeks until I could see that the best times were always when you were along. You were the best part of us. Soon, I couldn't see Portia in the equation anymore. I could only see you and me."

"I promise, Owen. I had no intention of—"

"Of course not. Neither did I. But Claire, you and I *work*. We fit."

She nestled closer. Everything about them fit. "I am happiest when I'm with you," she whispered, her voice hitching. "When I thought you were going to leave, I was bereft. Over the loss of your friendship, companionship, humor—the loss of you." Not to mention his touch, his kiss, his embrace. Though those were new, they had immediately become indispensable.

"I couldn't leave Sugarplum Falls, but more—I couldn't leave you." Owen lifted her chin and gazed down into her face.

Owen chose me. He loves me. She was aching to kiss him, to show him her feelings—without the play-acting factor involved.

He smiled. "You made me almost forget I have a hillside to show you."

The kiss would wait.

The lights stretched out before them, and they went on and on—for acres. "Whoa, Owen. When I said add a few more concentric circles of lighted trees, I wasn't picturing anything on this scale." The vast expanse of twinkling color spread all around them. "So much work."

193

"We needed it. I think the fact we agreed to work on the orchard is what allowed us to sing to Dad. The singing, I'm convinced, is what brought him back from wherever he was."

Claire gulped. "Without the meeting you called … then?"

"Then we wouldn't have my dad with us like this for Christmas." Owen stopped beneath the branches of a tree lit from trunk to branch-tips with white lights. "Our family has you to thank for it."

"Owen, I—" Claire's voice hitched. "I'm just so happy that your family is happy. Are you … okay? You and your dad?"

Owen nodded and they walked on a little way into the orchard. "We had a long talk." He took her hand. Owen stood a head taller, and his face was lit by the glow of the Christmas lights. Now, who looked like the angel? "In the process, we forgave each other."

Owen paused beneath a white-glowing lighted tree. He turned to face her, and his eyes were aglow with merriment.

"So, Claire Downing. How about you complete your mother's challenge?" He edged closer.

"Not that again." Claire groaned. "Isn't the supper club, starring in the play, making a zillion costumes, making new friends at the quilting club, and even putting my Claire Originals up for sale enough? When does it end?"

Owen stopped her argument with a kiss. His lips brushed hers, like an angel's robe's sleeve had grazed her skin. Gentle. Only a whisper of a touch.

Then, he kissed her in earnest.

Oh, goodness. That kiss was bottled reality—and hope and promise. It shook her very moorings, in all the best ways. *I love him.*

Her heart revved like a sewing machine with the pedal stuck at full speed. The kiss increased in speed and intensity. It was definitely something new. The kiss was going somewhere. The kiss was taking her into a new future.

"Oh, Owen." Claire pulled back before kissing him again. The newness of each pass of their lips was a revelation. A prophecy.

At last, Owen relinquished her. "I like the way you accept new challenges."

"What do you mean?" Oh, the kiss.

194

"How about one more new thing."

If it was anything like that kiss, she was all for it.

"How about becoming my girlfriend?"

Claire bit her lower lip, looking into his eyes. "I'd love to." She placed a soft, tender kiss on his mouth. "And for the record, kissing you will never get old."

"Owen!" Ellis ran down the path toward them on his short little legs. "I found you!"

Claire felt the same way. She could have shouted that phrase into the great night sky.

"Aunt Karma and Uncle Chug said we can't start the sledding until you and your fiancée get to the hill."

"Fiancée? Well, that escalated quickly." Owen laughed, grasping her hand.

He hadn't refuted the kid's title for her. "What else new is happening tonight, Owen Kingston?"

"The sledding hillside will tell."

They made their way to the newly reinstated annual sledding party for the Kingston family. Spice doughnuts, apple cider, and hot cocoa for everyone.

Everyone, including Claire.

"One of the best side-effects of the tree lighting is that we can sled at night for the first time," little Ellis said, jumping up and down and grabbing Claire's hand before running off to his sledding again.

"Are you ready for this?"

"If it's with you, I'm ready, Owen. She leaned against him on their toboggan. "Let's take things fast." They careened down the hill. "Is that a *double-entendre*?"

It just might have been.

Chapter 29

Claire

Claire laced her fingers through Owen's as they navigated the icy walkway up to the doors of the Kingston Theater. Opening night pulsated with energy. This year, they had a three-night run planned—just like last year's three-night sell-out. Funny how quickly two years had passed since she and Owen had been up on that stage.

In fact, this time around, Mom and Eddy were in the cast. Once they moved back to Sugarplum Falls this past summer, they'd dived into the Sugarplum Falls community in a huge way. Both would be wearing costumes from the stash of Victorian costumes Claire and the Kingston Kutters had made during that crazy month.

Claire missed living in the house where she grew up, and where she and Owen had called home since their marriage, but when Mom moved back, it was finally time for Claire to move on.

Now, Owen had built them a new one near the orchard.

With a nursery.

"The Orchard Walk is quite the hit this year. It was a good idea to allow sledding for anyone who wants to afterward." Owen squeezed her to his side. "You have the best ideas. The whole family loves you."

"Your mom makes the best spice doughnuts. Everyone is going to love them. Night sledding is the best." She'd learned that last year by the midnight sledding party with Owen's family. She and Owen had done a few additional sledding runs, just the two of them, since then. It might be her favorite sport—after kissing Owen. Which, yeah. That counted as a sport, considering how much cardio it ended up causing. "Do you think the guest Evangeline will be who we think it will?"

That was Claire's version of a joke. The Evangeline role this year was supposed to be a big secret surprise for everyone, but the illustrious Portia

Sutherland hadn't hesitated to post it all over her social media accounts that she and Archie would be returning to their roots for a special, two-night appearance in a nostalgic production.

"What I think, honestly, is that Fletch Fletcher was a genius to get her to come back and play the role." Owen handed their tickets to the usher. "When Mayor Lang tapped him to be the play's director, I thought she'd finally gone around the bend, but ..."

But it had turned out to be exactly what Fletch needed. The responsibility had pulled him up a level, and he'd reportedly done nothing to embarrass anyone sensitive to inappropriate comments. Plus, it hadn't hurt that he'd been sober ever since that Christmastime stint in rehab. The guy was going to be all right.

"My favorite casting decision," Claire said she waddled after Owen, "was Rex Peters as Nicholas."

"Oh, don't for a minute believe that was Fletcher's idea. That was all Mayor Lang."

The matchmaking mayor? "You're saying the mayor is trying to get Rex together with his costar?"

"You watch. By Valentine's Day, I'd wager good money Rex Peters and Marie Gatwick are engaged."

"Why, that scheming mayor." Sugarplum Falls had elected one of a kind as their leader. "Of course, I'd be really happy for them, no matter who'd pulled the strings."

"You think engagement is a good thing?"

"It's nowhere near as great as marriage." Marriage to Owen was incredible. Claire was the luckiest wife alive. "Oh, no. I'm not even going to fit into the seat." Claire let Owen tug her down the aisle of the theater slowly. She was practically a dirigible. "These chairs aren't made for the ready-to-burst pregnant woman."

They squeezed into the row, and Owen sat in the second seat, leaving the aisle for her.

"Then you can sit on my lap." Owen pulled her down onto him. "You're comfortable here, I take it."

197

"Owen!" Claire sank against him, ignoring the cramp in her stomach. "We're in public."

"We had our first public display of affection here, so what's one more?" Owen allowed her to scoot over into her own place, but he draped an arm over her shoulders. "Can you believe it was only two years ago?"

"Time must go faster for you since you're not the pregnant one." But truthfully, it seemed like yesterday Claire had been in tears on that stage, thinking Owen was going to leave her forever. "Of course, I wouldn't trade a single moment of it."

"Especially the get-pregnant moment."

"Owen!" Claire buried her face in his shoulder. "We're not alone here. There are kids all around us."

"Yes, and their mothers had to be pregnant at some point or other for that to be the case."

He was incorrigible.

Up walked Mayor Lang. "Claire! Owen!" She leaned in and hugged Claire. "You're as gorgeous as ever. And the baby? What will you call her?"

How did Mayor Lang know baby was a girl? Well, Mayor Lang made it her business to know these things. "We're thinking of Portia. For her godmother."

"Oh, I can just see the thrill on my Sutherland niece's face at that." Mayor Lang smiled broadly. "And I assume you've got matching custom dresses for you and Baby Portia in every size from newborn on up? That mother-daughter dress business of yours might suffer while you're on maternity leave. I hope you've budgeted for that."

"Lulu is running the store like a champ, as always." Owen nudged his way in. "And the Kingston Kutters are taking over all the custom sewing projects while Claire is caring for the baby."

"Isn't it nice to have family?" Mayor Lang moved on.

Yeah, it was nice to have family. Lots of family.

"Oh, dear." Speaking of family. Someone was wanting to join it a couple of weeks sooner than her due date. One giant contraction hit her, and it meant business. "Owen? I'm afraid we're going to miss the final stage kiss."

"But, we told Portia and Archie we'd—"

"Have someone video it for us." She turned to him. "Owen. It's time."

Owen's eyes flew wide. "As in *time* time?"

"Time to meet the newest Kingston."

He took her by the hand, and they headed into the biggest new adventure of both their lives. Together.

Epilogue

Cliff Rockingham

Cliff Rockingham's feet pounded on the frozen ground of the jogging trail near the roaring waterfall while his brain roared even louder.

What am I going to do?

His soul *needed* Christmas giving—in a *real* way. Toy drives and groceries and gift certificates for those in need in Sugarplum Falls hadn't cut it last year, or the year before, or the year before.

No, it's got to be deeply meaningful this year. Not just changing a holiday morning. Changing a *life*.

But what? And for whom?

Cliff rounded the corner of the jogging trail where the waterfall came into view—his favorite sight, Falls Overlook. The view of Lake Sugar, stretching to the western horizon, with the waterfall spilling off the lake's southern edge, was famously inspiring.

Cliff needed inspiring, since even being on his roof hadn't helped him think. Maybe the view would inspire him to—

His train of thought screeched to a halt.

Someone was already standing at the Falls Overlook. And—wait a second! What was she doing? That was dangerous.

"Hey!" He picked up speed. "Hold up!" He ran faster, his thighs catching fire.

Don't jump!

A young woman leaned precariously over the railing protecting Falls Overlookers from the churning waters below. Her blonde hair lifted in the breeze while her arm arched backward, as if giving herself momentum to dive.

"Stop!" he cried, breaking into a dead run.

"I've got you!" Cliff reached her side and yanked her backward, toppling

200

both of them—but not before a blue cylinder flew from her hand, soaring toward the frigidly cold lake below.

Oof! They smacked onto the ground, but the woman was safe! Cliff clutched her to his chest, his breath coming in heaves.

"Are you okay?" Cliff pushed himself to his feet and pleaded with her. "Whatever is going on in your life, it's not as bad as it seems right now. Things always get better."

He reached to help her stand, taking in her appearance. She looked *very* familiar, but he couldn't place her. Soft, feminine features, natural and without makeup. With her straight blonde hair that glinted in the winter sunlight, she could've been an actress.

She accepted his help and stood, dusting herself off.

She definitely wasn't from Sugarplum Falls. He would've noticed. The stunner had to be a tourist. Sugarplum Falls couldn't keep a secret as pretty as she was.

"Look, I get it. I've seen some dark days, too. They pass."

"I was"—she squeezed her hands into fists—"just looking at the lake." The tourist's honey-brown eyes stared back at him in pure annoyance.

Hey, what was with that reaction? He'd saved her life!

Most other people might have said that her lake-leaning was none of his business, but Cliff lived by Jacob Marley of Dickensian literature's maxim, *Mankind was my business!*

"Well, the lake is prettier when it freezes solid." *But that would hurt even more if you plunged into it, so don't.*

"I bet it is." She glanced over the railing, her fair hair catching a breeze, lifting and falling—her frown deepening and revealing more complex feelings churning inside her than sightseeing. "I'm sure you meant well."

Uh, of course he'd meant well! "I'm just glad you're safe."

"Safe's a relative term." She gave him a little, sad smile, while rubbing her shoulder. "Well, bye." She stepped around him and headed toward the parking lot.

Cliff, being a dingbat, tagged along after her. "Where are you staying?"

"At the Gingerbread Inn."

"Really? Gingerbread Inn?" Not *that* place! *Why not Sweetwater Hotel?* Argh!

"You've heard of Gingerbread Inn?"

Yup. He'd heard of it. He'd wanted to pull his hair out because of it.

"Newly remodeled place on Orchard?" The kitschy, boutique lodges in Sugarplum Falls were killing him—and his business, Sweetwater Hotel—especially Gingerbread Inn. "Sure. This is a small town."

Maybe I should offer her a free night's stay at Sweetwater Hotel. Show her what she's missing. Except that would sound like a pickup line. Maybe even a creepy one.

"You look like you just choked on a candy cane." She paused beside a red jeep. "Is there something wrong with Gingerbread Inn?"

Her phone chimed a holiday ring-tone—the song "I Heard the Bells on Christmas Day"—cutting off his reply about Gingerbread Inn and the bed and breakfasts popping up around town—with their low ceilings, their cramped rooms, and their dark, fairytale cottage vibes—being signs of the End Times for Sweetwater Hotel, the premier lodging in Sugarplum Falls.

"A little dreary for a ring tone," he commented instead.

"It's my alarm." She pulled it out and shut off the tune of the Wordsworth poem's song. "Gotta go. It's almost check-in time at the inn."

She climbed into the jeep and started the engine.

Wait. Was she really leaving? But—but, he hadn't gotten her name, even.

She rolled down the window halfway. "Have a good day." She gave him a partial smile. "Sorry for getting upset when you tackled me. I know you were just being a knight in shining armor."

Mercy! The radiant sunshine of even that small smile could've melted the iceberg that sank the *Titanic.*

The jeep began to back up, but Cliff put his hand on the door's frame, as if he could keep her from driving off by sheer force of will. "What's your name?"

"It's Sam-Jessamyn."

"Sorry?" *It's I'm Jessamyn?* Is that what she'd said? "I'm Cliff Rockingham." He offered his full name. "It was nice meeting you, Jessamyn

…" Hint, hint. *Give me your last name?*

But why? So that he could … what? Internet stalk her?

I do not stalk. Not women who look like movie stars. Not blondes with honey-brown eyes. And especially not tourists. Tourists are temporary. I'm permanent.

"Bye, Cliff Rockingham." The window swished upward. He stepped back so the jeep wouldn't run over his foot. The jeep disappeared down Orchard Street.

A countdown clock began ticking down the hours and minutes until he could see her again, until he could try to be her knight in shining armor again.

No! He yanked the battery out of that dumb countdown clock. He didn't crush on tourists. Tourists, by their very definition, didn't stay.

And Cliff had had far more than his share of impermanent relationships.

Read the rest of Cliff Rockingham and Jessamyn Fleet's exciting love story with a tiny twist of suspense. Grab Christmas at Gingerbread Inn *and fall in love one more time at snowy, Christmastime Sugarplum Falls, as Cliff secretly answers a desperate message in a bottle letter addressed to Santa Claus—and gets in over his head with a sweet rival hotel owner who is keeping a terrible secret.*

Author's Note

All stories in the Sugarplum Falls Romance series are clean, standalone holiday romances. **They're arranged in a loop**. Book 1 introduces characters from book 2, and so forth, until *Christmas at Gingerbread Inn* loops back to *Christmas at Holly Berry Cottage*. This means readers can begin at any point in the series and then complete the loop to fall in love over and over, while meeting the many recurring characters from the familiar and charming small town of Sugarplum Falls.

The Sugarplum Falls Romance Series

Christmas at Holly Berry Cottage
Christmas at Turtledove Place
Christmas at Angels Landing
Christmas at Sugarplum Falls
Christmas at Gingerbread Inn

For a short and sweet Sugarplum Falls Christmas romance, sign up for Jennifer's bubbly newsletter and receive *Christmas at The Cider Press* as an ebook for free. Email her at jennifergriffithauthor@yahoo.com and ask for the link.

Jennifer's other sweet holiday romance series include the Christmas House Romances, Snowfall Wishes, plus several standalone sweet holiday novels, and lots of romantic comedies set at other times of the year. Check out all her books on Amazon.

About the Author

J ennifer Griffith lives in Arizona with her husband, where they are raising their five children to love Christmas. She tries to put more lights on her tree each year, and she wholeheartedly believes the best way to kick off the holiday season is to sing Christmas songs with her husband's extended family for two to three hours on Thanksgiving night. Her favorite carol is "O Holy Night," and her favorite Christmas song is "Walking in a Winter Wonderland." She once sang a contralto solo of "Gesu Bambino" that wasn't too bad. The best part of it was her oldest son accompanied her on the piano.

Made in the USA
Middletown, DE
11 August 2024

58912617R00128